DIED
ON A
RAINY
SUNDAY

JOAN AIKEN

DIED ON A RAINY SUNDAY

HOLT, RINEHART AND WINSTON

NEW YORK   CHICAGO   SAN FRANCISCO

BOOKS BY JOAN AIKEN

FOR YOUNG READERS

Died on a Rainy Sunday
The Cuckoo Tree
The Green Flash
Night Fall
Smoke from Cromwell's Time
A Necklace of Raindrops
The Whispering Mountain
Armitage, Armitage, Fly Away Home
Nightbirds on Nantucket
Black Hearts in Battersea
The Wolves of Willoughby Chase

FOR ADULTS

The Embroidered Sunset
The Crystal Crow
The Fortune Hunters
Dark Interval
Beware of the Bouquet
The Silence of Herondale

. . . BUT IT RAINED EVERY SUNDAY THAT summer, and on most weekdays too. The grass on the slopes surrounding the new house grew long, bright green, and frail; sodden puddles of browning chestnut blossom lay drifted along the edges of the village street; the porch rapidly became cluttered with damp gumboots and rusting metal toys. The plaster on the inside walls dried slowly and patchily, and the paint sweated; any surface, however recently wiped, felt damp and slightly greasy to the touch. At night rain dripped, hour after wakeful hour, on the carefully chosen, carefully matched roof tiles; Jane, lying, listening to it, remembered some documentary film she had seen about pygmies; the sound resembled approaching tiny drums. The house, with no dust yet drifted to rest in its interstices, no insulating layers of fluff, was a hollow sounding-box, and amplified any tick or clink

1

made inside it to the proportions of radio melodrama. Voices boomed; the slightest remark assumed an ominous significance.

Every day the postman, draped in glistening black plastic, grumbled bitterly to himself as he splashed down the long, puddled drive, and demanded of Providence why the Drummonds had chosen to build their house half hidden behind trees at the farthest possible distance from the road.

Jane Drummond jumped out of bed one Monday morning, after a restless night, and ran down the polished pine stairs, her cotton housecoat swishing coldly around her bare legs, to stoke the fine new stove.

Her shining house was morning-calm under its veil of rain; Graham still asleep, so was the baby; only from Caroline's room drifted a subdued, tuneless humming.

Plum, the Siamese, came stretching and yawning from his basket, flexed his back legs, then his front, then rubbed himself against Jane's ankles; absently she fondled his silky dark-brown head, stooping to pick up the heap of bills that lay on the front-door mat—two of them, she noticed, marked Final Demand.

At the bottom of the pile was one real letter: square, white, typed, London postmark, addressed to herself, Mrs. Jane Dillon Drummond, Weir View House, Culveden, Kent. Now, who?. . .

She put it aside to keep till after breakfast, and started making the porridge.

Her mind ran along its accustomed groove.

Bills. Sell something? Nothing worth selling. Get a job? But I swore I wouldn't till Donald was five at least. Four and a half years to go. Try to get freelance work at home . . . reading scripts? Editing them? Yes, maybe, but poorly paid. And we need a lot of

2

money *now*. Still, I'll write to Folia—today—no harm
making a start. What else? Enter Why-I-Like-Krunchy-
Choc-Bars competition. Do football pools. Buy a pre-
mium bond. Go on the streets. Invest five pounds in
a platinum-mine company. Get run over and sue someone for huge damages. Be recognized as potential star
material by a foreign film director who happens to be
strolling through Culveden.

The porridge boiled; she stirred it and moved it to
the side of the hot plate.

GRAHAM WAS UNWONTEDLY CHEERFUL AT BREAKFAST, IG-
noring the bills.

"I met your friend Tom Roland in the pub last
night," he said, eating his porridge, walking about in
ostentatiously Scots style, pausing to admire the Dutch
dresser, with its load of china and glassware that
needed to be dusted every four days.

A fourth visit to the pub in two weeks? Graham was
usually a sparse drinker, because of his ulcer; so what
was this?

"Hardly my friend," Jane countered mildly, and
went on cutting bread-and-butter fingers for Caroline,
sprinkling them with brown sugar. "Work on a script
for a couple of months, five years ago, hardly qualifies
as friendship. . . ."

"Well, anyway, *he* remembered *you*. He lives down
here. Has the converted oast house halfway up the hill.
. . . Carey and Wing did the conversion for him, he
told me. Nice job; he invited me to go in and look at
it sometime. I bought him a drink—"

Graham stopped abruptly and scrutinized one of the tiles in the black-and-red checkerboard floor. Jane had time to think, If this goes on, it's not going to do Graham's ulcer any good, before he resumed, satisfied that the tile was in good condition, "Tom'll be a useful chap to have as a friend around here—definitely the local celebrity. He has heaps of TV people down at weekends, Miss Ames told me; sometimes she puts up the overflow in her guest house. Might be some handy contacts—people who decide they want a weekend cottage built, or converted. I've invited Tom to come and take a look at this house whenever he likes."

Damn, Jane thought. That means bandbox perfection all the time, not a toy on the floor, or it'll be, "Suppose Tom Roland were to drop in?"

Why did I let myself be persuaded to leave our perfectly adequate suburban flat and move to this place? Did he know Tom Roland lived here? Was Roland the real governing factor behind Graham's insistence on building his house in Culveden? The fact that I'd once worked with him briefly and could claim acquaintance?

Graham's motives were often secretively hoarded, revealed slowly, piecemeal, as it suited him, or when necessity obliged him.

She looked at her husband dispassionately. After six years of marriage she could afford to be dispassionate. But grant him his appearance: slight, dark, and almost excessively handsome, he could have posed in lovelocks and ruffles for a portrait of the Young Chevalier.

He was by the window, drumming his fingers impatiently on the red-tiled sill, disapproving of the rain that was making his lawn grass grow long and spindly.

"Have we any bananas?" he asked suddenly.

"No, we haven't. Why?"

"I wouldn't mind one."

"Now?"

Graham never, in any circumstances, ate anything but porridge, tea, and a four-minute boiled egg for breakfast; any variation from this routine he would previously have regarded as uncivilized, un-British, eccentric, downright barbarian.

"Tom always has three bananas for breakfast; he told me."

Tom this, Tom that. Are we to expect him for breakfast? she wondered.

She gave Graham his boiled egg, brown toast, and opened her letter. Plum jumped on to her lap unreproved and began to purr: a loud, joyful rumble not unlike the roar of the weir which, after so many nights of rain, made a distant, continuous accompaniment audible above and through every nearer sound.

". . . Goodness!"

"What is it?" Graham's voice was indulgent.

"It's from Folia Films. Funny, I was just thinking about them. They want me to go back for a couple of months; Sandy Wilshaw's in hospital with a kidney thing. They're doing a documentary on British porcelain. They've got all the material; they just want me to work on the script. They're offering three hundred. But I don't see how I can."

She sounded shocked. *Three hundred,* she thought. The coal bill, the gas bill, the grocery bill, the removal bill, the telephone bill, the garage bill . . . slipcovers . . . a pushchair . . . children's summer clothes. . . . There might even be ten pounds left to make myself some cotton dresses, supposing the sun's ever going to come out again.

"Can't you do the work at home, if they've got all the stuff collected?" Graham's attention was thoroughly engaged now.

"No. Folia doesn't work that way. It's all trial and

error; I'd simply have to be there for script conferences.''

"Well, then, of course you must go back. After all, Donald's six months old now, and as sturdy as a pony, bless him. You could stop feeding him yourself. There are such things as bottles.''

All psychology reared its heads at her, like the Hydra: deprivation, loss, infantile trauma. . . .

But is it worse to lose your mother for a few hours each day for a couple of months, or to have a mother who is never for a moment free from desperate worry? What is one to do?

And it was true that Donald was a sturdy, placid baby, with a great propensity for sleep. Caroline might be the one to suffer. . . .

"Anyway,'' she said, grasping at straws, "who could we possibly find to look after him and Caroline? We don't know a soul except Miss Ames, and she's too busy with her guest house and her café—''

"Oh, we'd find somebody. Easily. Miss Ames could probably suggest a woman. There's sure to be someone or other in the village who'd be glad to earn some extra cash for a couple of months.''

Just someone or other won't do to look after my Donald and Caroline, Jane thought, wiping Caroline's milky face, setting her free from her bib and chair.

"Run along upstairs, my precious. I'll be up in two ticks.''

"And we can do with the money,'' Graham said clinchingly.

You're telling me we can do with it, she cried at him silently; but he was grandly ignoring the Final Demands.

"As a matter of fact it will come in nicely,'' he said. "I was just going to tell you that I bought Tom

6

Roland's Hovermow off him last night—he let me have it for two hundred. And I owe a bit to old Saunders at the office; had to borrow it last week when I was a bit short."

Sick despair was such a familiar sensation that Jane took a steady pull at her good, hot coffee before she answered, "You bought a power mower? Why did you do that? What's wrong with the one we have?"

"*Why?*" He seemed puzzled at her stupidity. "Well, of course we've got to have a decent sweep of lawn all around this place to show it off properly. Impress clients. And you can't do those slopes properly with the old mower. Don't you understand yet? This house has to be a showpiece: my own place, all designed and executed by me."

All on borrowed money.

"But I can't use a Hovermow," Jane said quietly. "They're too heavy for me. The old mower suits me fine. After all, I'm the one who does the job."

Graham waved aside the slight dryness in her tone. "My dear child," he said impatiently, "that old machine was in a hopeless state. Anyway you shouldn't be cutting the grass—it doesn't look too good. Miss Ames said people in the village have been commenting about it. So I'm getting a chap to come in twice a week and do the garden. Tom told me about him—he works for Tom two days a week as well, so he can easily fit us in. Tom's going to speak to him today and tell him to come around here and discuss times."

And what are we going to pay him with? Blueprints?

She didn't say it. She had brought not saying things to a fine art. She stacked the breakfast dishes; she mixed cereal for the baby's morning feed.

"Come to think," Graham said, "this gardening chap—don't know his name, Tom forgot to mention it,

7

but he lives down at the bottom of the village—he has a wife who sometimes washes up for Roland when he has one of his parties. Very likely she'd take the kids on for a couple of months—maybe she has some of her own. We certainly need that three hundred, can't afford to let such a windfall go. You write to Folia and accept—when do they want you?''

"First of next month."

"Oh, well, there's plenty of time to find somebody then. I'll ask this gardening bloke when I interview him, and maybe put it around in the pub—that's the way to get things fixed in a village," Graham said knowledgeably. "And you ask Miss Ames. Okay, see you this evening—lots of work, I'll probably be late again—''

He stood up, stretched, and prepared to go off to his beautifully decorated office. As an afterthought he dropped a kiss on Jane's ear; she was looking down at the pile of unopened envelopes.

Graham paused in the porch, and ran a proud, caressing hand over the head of his baby son, who slept there; then, giving a critical glance at the landscaped but still semiwild garden, he walked briskly around to the garage.

After a moment or two Jane started on her morning round of tasks.

When she had finished the baby's ten-o'clock feed, she looked thoughtfully down at him: nearly asleep, utterly content, the human cocoon, his absurd, foreshortened face with one drop of milk clinging to a downy cheek already abstracted, folded into a Buddhist calm. She settled him back in his carry-cot, and he sighed like an adult, his arms immediately rising into their accustomed position, up on each side of his face, fists clenched. Why did babies double their fists, even when apparently relaxed? Was it because of the struggle they knew must lie ahead, or the struggle to be born that already lay behind them?

As she set the cot back on the porch, wafts of rain slapped against the glassed-in walls, the brick floor was dark with moisture. She clipped the waterproof cover over Donald's blue blanket.

Beyond the porch there was total silence. Rain dripped; birds thought their own thoughts.

At this hour in an office morning, mail would be arriving, meetings being held, coffee drunk, phones ringing. . . . Suddenly she knelt and laid her face by Donald's sleeping one.

Next moment she rose briskly and went back indoors. The beds were still waiting, so was Donald's daily wash; there was a shopping list to be made out. Caroline was happily occupied in floating wooden cotton spools in a plastic dish tub on the kitchen floor; the charm of playing with water never failed. The front of her sweater was already soaked, but there was no sense in changing it until she tired and moved on to some other occupation.

Anyway, Jane thought, if Graham insists on this gardener coming to work for us, I'll ask him to get those fences down at the bottom of the garden fixed. I know Caroline hasn't made her way down there yet, but sooner or later she's bound to, and although the fence looks all right, half the stakes are rotted through, and with the weir only two fields away one can't be too careful.

The solid roar of the swollen weir made itself heard again as the spin dryer whirred to a halt.

Jane rolled the dryer into its niche, scanned the larder, made out the grocery list, and dressed herself and Caroline to go down to the village. Take Donald?

No, leave him. He slept peacefully; they would be gone only ten minutes, twelve at most. And nobody came to the house; they knew no one as yet. Graham was not one for casual friendships; all his dealings had a purpose.

Culveden village was set like a watercourse winding down a hillside. Ancient little houses were settled into folds of the hill as if they had been lodged there in some centuries-bygone flood. Massive trees marked the bends in the road; it was not a hill to take at speed, going either way.

The rain was blowing in mild, cloudy drifts, hardly distinguishable from the smoke wavering up from the irregularly placed chimneys. Few people were out so early on an unpromising morning, but one figure came striding in their direction along the narrow twisting street.

Bother, said Jane to herself, and determinedly crossed to the post office, with its three worn stone steps and cheerful red letterbox.

A shout from behind brought her to a halt. "Janey! *Janey!*"

"Who's that man calling you Janey, mother?" said Caroline interestedly.

"Oh, hullo," Jane said, accepting defeat.

"Didn't you remember me?"

"Of course, I did. But I didn't think you'd remember *me.*"

Tom Roland looked down at her, smiling. He was an immense creature; she had forgotten how tall he was, even in proportion to his breadth—damn it, after all it *had* been five years ago, for two months only, if that —with unruly dark hair, lively dark eyes, wide mobile mouth, a habit of vigorous Gallic gesture, and a pipe that, to the delight of countless TV viewers, never would stay lit.

10

He rapped it against the post-office wall and stuck it in his pocket.

"You haven't changed a bit," he said, surveying her with approval. "Do you remember that awful day at the railway siding when the film hadn't come and the east wind never stopped blowing and we all huddled into a cattle truck and played twenty-one with a pack that had only forty-nine cards and two of them blew into a water tank?"

"Vividly."

But what a memory he had; after all, his life must have been piled high with such experiences.

"And we didn't finish filming till ten to eleven and got to a pub just before closing time, and they made us cocoa with rum in it. You and I had a discussion about the things we hated; you said laundry string, and I said those squashy cheeses in silver foil they serve on airliners that one can never get open. And you said the young man who's always smiling fondly over the girl's shoulder in ad pictures. And I said—"

Oh, no, Jane cried out in silent protest. How could she not remember?

That had been the last day's filming. Luckily. Of course it had meant nothing, but for weeks after that evening, that lighthearted exchange, easy as a running brook, she had gone about in a curious numbness, as if a limb had been amputated and the anaesthetic had not yet worn off, feeling that she communicated with Graham in Sanskrit, Urdu, deaf-and-dumb talk. Laundry string, she could imagine Graham saying, why the devil *laundry string*?

And she had only been married nine months then.

Tom had rung the office—that was when she was still full-time with Folia—two or three times, suggesting lunch or a drink, but she had been evasive, noncommittal; really she hadn't dared see him any more.

11

She had not mentioned the calls to Graham, or he would certainly have insisted on her inviting Tom back to the apartment. At that time Roland was just becoming well known for his part in the panel game *Curio Comic*. As it was, for months Graham had gone about proudly saying, "My wife's been working with Tom Roland on a film about British railway architecture; *the* Tom Roland—you know, the one who's a design expert and appears on that TV quiz program. She knows him quite well."

In a way it was pathetic.

Luckily then, Tom had gone off to Copenhagen on some project, and a month or two afterwards, Jane had stopped full-time work, with Caroline on the way; and that was that, she had thought with relief.

". . . And oddly enough there's a perfect specimen living in this very village. The moment I first saw her I thought of you, Janey. Do you remember? You said you couldn't stand little women in jersey suits with prim buttoned-up faces and curly brown hair called Hazel or Myfanwy. I almost sent you a postcard—if I'd known your address I would have—she's so exactly to specification. I just can't wait for you to see her, must try to arrange it somehow.

"Your daughter's summing me up," he broke off to say. He nodded in a friendly way at Caroline, who, with her orange rain hood pushed back off her ragged fringe of dark hair, was scowling at him, in concentration, not dislike.

"Hullo. My name's Tom. What's yours?"

But Caroline was mute with strangers.

"Who's that particular man, mother?" she said aside. *Particular* was her word at present; last week it had been *suitable*.

"An old friend, precious."

"Not all *that* old," said Caroline judicially.

"Your daughter's no silvery fairy-tale mouse. Not like you—I can see she's got plenty of Boadicea in her. Oh, by the way, I met your husband in the Swan last night. Did he tell you? It's queer; somehow I find it hard to envisage him as your husband. And yet you must have been married already when I knew you before. Some people one never thinks of as married. Actually I feel rather guilty because I sold him my old Hovermow, or rather, he seemed dead keen to buy it off me, though I was complaining about it. I don't usually start my friendships by flogging things to people. Still, it does cut grass; it's just rather heavy."

"Oh, but he's thrilled about it," Jane said swiftly. "A mower that's belonged to Tom Roland—that's practically the equivalent of Irving's dagger. He'll be able to boast to everyone about it."

As the words left her, she thought with horror, Why did I say that? How cheap, how stupid it sounds. She saw the hurt in Tom's eyes and told herself in panic, No! I'm not going to feel that way again.

"I'm sorry," she said swiftly, "that was mean and uncalled-for. No, we really do need a better mower than the old thing we've got; the grass is almost up to our ears. And what with moving in, and new furniture, and so forth, we certainly couldn't afford to buy a new one."

"We are going to be good neighbors, aren't we, Janey? Friends?"

"Of course. . . . Of course we are."

His face was like a romantic landscape, she thought. A picture by Géricault, light and shade, a great deal going on. It broke into a smile of relief at hers.

"We must fly home now," she said hurriedly. "I left the baby sleeping on the porch; I didn't reckon to be

13

gone more than ten minutes. People will be thinking I'm a most negligent mother, wondering what I've done with him. You know how it is in a village: that Mrs. Drummond just goes out shopping and leaves her baby; she's got no help in the house, I know, and her husband leaves for business every morning at half past eight; poor little mite left all on his own in the house; someone ought to tell the N.S.P.C.C. about it.''

"Too much imagination, Janey," he said, laughing. "That was always your trouble."

As she moved away, she noticed somebody watching them both intently through the steamy pane of the post-office window. An avid, gimlet-eyed stare.

BACK HOME FOR HIS NOONDAY MEAL, TIM MC GREGOR PULLED off the dirty old commando beret (which he had no shadow of right to wear), dropped it on the TV, flung himself into a wicker chair whose grubby cushions fitted him like a plaster cast, and waited for Myfanwy to bring in the potatoes.

He had a piece of news for her.

The tiny bungalow stood somewhat removed from the other houses, down at the bottom of the village. Built on a piece of marshland in the between-war days before planning regulations were strictly enforced, it was a last-hope dwelling, with paper-thin walls, without a damp-course; nobody who could afford anything better, or who wanted to stay alive, uncrippled by rheumatism, stayed in it a week longer than they could help. There was also a sporting chance that if the weir should ever overflow *Mon Abri*—which was what

14

ironically it was called—would be engulfed in the flood.

For these reasons the rent was quite low.

The whole house smelled of drains, or the lack of them. It was running with damp, and so dark from the elder bushes surrounding it, that its full squalor could only be guessed at; all a casual observer would have received was an over-all impression of rags, rust, peeling wallpaper, and the smell of potatoes burned daily in old, thin saucepans.

The only clean object in the place was little Susan, who sat stolidly in her highchair, in her pink organdy frock, with two pink plastic butterflies in her hair, clean white socks and clean red strap shoes on her feet, looking at nothing.

Four years ago, at the age of two, little Susan had been for one blissful, unbelievable year a Cover Girl; she had been Discovered, through the process of winning the competition run by Sugarbaby Soap, as the Bonniest Baby of the Season. (Her mother had sent in her snapshot, with a soap wrapper.)

It had been like a dream. . . . For a whole year, money had poured into the McGregor househould (which could do with it, just then); little Susan's face had appeared, rapt in babyish solemnity, in full color on the front covers of *Mother Magazine, Woman's World, Ladies' Look* and even *Saturday Mail,* gazing at a butterfly, blowing bubbles, smiling at a kitten. She had appeared on TV, on hoardings, even on cereal packages.

For one whole year the glory had lasted; then little Susan's raptness and solemnity had somehow jelled, turned fatally to stolidity; and now she was thick-set, overfed on high-calorie food, and expressionless as a pudding made of brick. Nobody wanted her any more. The wayward fancy of ad agencies had turned elsewhere. But Susan's mother still could not believe that

15

those days had gone for ever, would never return; nor that the decline in little Susan's popularity had come about through the course of nature, and not by the malice of enemies.

She still took snapshots of Susan regularly—even if they had to go without necessities, she had Susan's hair done at the hairdresser's—sometimes had studio photographs taken, sending them off to agencies, which no longer bothered to reply.

"Hurry up with the grub, Myfanwy," shouted Tim irritably. "I haven't got all day."

Myfanwy brought in the dinner without replying, merely pressing her lips together. She did not look at her husband, but kept her eyes fixed on the dish of potatoes she was setting down on the plastic lace mat. She was a small, thin-skinned woman with a round face, tiny mouth, and protuberant pale-gray eyes—quick, darting eyes that missed nothing. She had a faint, dark, downy moustache, and there were freckles on her hands. She wore, from choice apparently, always the same shades of drab navy blue or dark brown; her clothes were the kind that it was hard to envisage anybody going into a shop and buying on purpose.

"Want to hear a joke, Myfanwy?" Tim said, pulling up a backless chair to the table.

She made no reply, still continued in her occupation of putting a plateful of potatoes and tinned peas in front of little Susan, mashing a bit of marge into the potato. Don't give me any jokes, don't bother *me* with your bits of chat, the resentful spark in her eyes, the set of her compressed mouth conveyed. I've got too many troubles of my own to be struck by anything *you* can tell me.

"Guess who's been building that new house up Copse Hill and just come to live in the village?" McGregor laughed, not loudly for he never did laugh aloud, but softly, in a contented chuckle, like the cat, hidden under the pantry shelf, watching the cream jug carried in. "And the funniest part of it all is, Roland's recommended me for the job of gardener there. Want a gardener, they do. Guess who it is."

"How should *I* know? How d'you expect me to guess?" Myfanwy said sharply, slapping down his plate in front of him.

So then he told her who had come to live up on Copse Hill.

BY FIVE IN THE EVENING, ALTHOUGH IT WAS SUMMER, THE weeping gray sky had settled down so low that Jane switched on all the lights. Extravagant, but the house seemed unchancy, apprehensive in the unnatural dusk. She put on a record of nursery rhymes in the sitting room for Caroline. The room, with its off-white curtains, pale carpet, and pale-green walls seemed like an aquarium with the wild, wet green vista outside the french windows; Jane wasn't certain whether she would have expected to see fish swimming inside or outside the glass.

She went upstairs and began somewhat ruefully surveying what remained of her office wardrobe— dresses five years the wrong length, jackets which, through lack of wear, were now a different shade from the skirts they were supposed to match.

Rain drove against the bedroom window; trees along the drive flailed and thrashed. No one's going to be able to cut the grass when it's like this, whatever they

17

use, Jane thought. Then, glancing up towards the front gate through blowing plumes of rain, she was astonished to see, as she thought, her husband coming home. What could have happened to the car? And why so early? Latterly Graham seldom arrived much before seven or even eight. Pressure of work on the big new private estate at Hastings.

Jane ran down and shoveled toys off the kitchen floor, swiftly slid together all the magazines from which Caroline had been cutting pictures. At any moment she expected to hear Graham's key in the lock.

Instead, after a longish pause—Had he lost his key? What was he *doing* out there?—she was disconcerted by a tap at the back door. Not a knock: a single, soft tap.

"Oh—" said Jane in surprise, opening the door. "How extr—I thought you were—I'm sorry. Come in, won't you, out of the wet?"

In her confusion, she was more welcoming than she would have been if she had had time to collect herself and fully observe the newcomer. She had an impression of someone gauntly thin, under the old black waterproof cape; of rumpled dark hair; narrow, bright, untrustworthy black eyes, and a sharp, metallic smell. Sweat? On this chilly damp evening?

The man had taken off his beret and held it in his hands.

"Good evening, madam." Even in her echoing kitchen his voice, with its unmistakable Highland intonation, was very soft, so soft that she could only just catch the words. "Thank you. Is the master—is Mr. Drummond at home? I've been sent round by Mr. Tom Roland. He said Mr. Drummond had some work in the garden that wanted doing, that he wished to speak with me about it."

"Oh," said Jane. "Are you—?" She hesitated. She did not know the man's name, and somehow the word *gardener,* so solid, rustic, and dependable, seemed utterly unsuited to this man. He did not in the least resemble her idea of a gardener, who ought to have a fringe of white beard and trousers tied up at the knee with bast.

"I'm McGregor, madam."

He waited a moment. Why did the silence seem ominous? McGregor, now, was a very proper name for a gardener, straight out of *Peter Rabbit.* And yet—and yet—Mr. McGregor's garden had been a place of mystery, a place where frightening things happened.

"Mr. Roland said Mr. Drummond wanted someone to come and do his outside work, regular."

Somehow he managed to invest the phrase "outside work" with a pejorative quality, to suggest that it was menial and degrading.

"Yes, he does," Jane said. "But I'm afraid my husband isn't back yet, Mr. McGregor."

She found herself quite unable to speak cordially or to smile at him. For a start, she disapproved so profoundly of hiring help that they could not afford. And then—it was stupid, irrational, but there was something that gave her the creeps about this man's thin, watchful presence, his dark vulpine face; something uncomfortable yet also, in a queer way, familiar. Why? She could not place the cause, yet felt instinctively antagonistic, like the sheep dog who sees a circling stranger approach his flock. McGregor seemed, as he stood humbly dripping in her warm, tidy kitchen, to smell faintly of the wild. He held the wet beret in his hands, looking down at it, hardly raising his eyes to Jane's; he hardly moved a step, as if fearing to drip on her waxed tiles; yet she had the impression that in

19

a couple of swift darting glances he had taken in the entire contents of the room and estimated their value, too.

The sound of music in the next room came to an end.

"Mummy?" Caroline wandered in, carrying, for some reason, one of Jane's few bits of family silver, a candlestick which she had recently become devoted to and christened Henry. "Mummy, my music's stopped."

"I'll come in a moment, precious, and turn it over. Go and switch off the switch now, can you?"

Jane felt a protective urge to hustle her daughter out of the stranger's company.

"Your little girl, madam?" said MacGregor respectfully. "Quite a little beauty, isn't she?" He gazed with apparent admiration at Caroline, but something else flickered in his eyes for a second. Jane told herself that her stupid, illogical hostility was making her hypercritical, was making her imagine things. No doubt it was all the result of guilt.

She wondered what to do. She had a strong impulse against leaving him alone in the room. But it would be uncivil to send him away, and not sensible; Graham must, surely, arrive any moment now. It was already well past Caroline's bedtime.

"Won't you sit down?" she said awkwardly. "My husband won't be long, I'm sure."

"I'll stand. Thank you, madam."

Why? What's wrong with our chairs?

But, of course, he was wet. It was pure consideration. The flickering notion that passed through her mind was childish nonsense.

"Oh, here's my husband now," she said in profound relief, hearing the unmistakable slam of the garage

20

door and then the crunch of Graham's step on the front path. She went swiftly into the hall as the front door opened, taking care to pull the kitchen door to behind her.

"The man Tom Roland sent has come," she murmured in an undertone. "He's in the kitchen."

"Oh, splendid." Graham shrugged off his raincoat and slung it over a hook. "Well"—glancing back through the glass panes of the front door—"there's not much he'll be able to get on with this evening, but I'll have a chat with him, tell him what I've planned for him to do. Have you asked him about his wife—whether she'd be willing to come and see to the kids here while you go back to Folia?"

"No, I haven't," she said, escaping. "He's only just come. You can do that."

And she went upstairs, shepherding Caroline before her, shut herself into the bathroom with the child, and turned the taps on full. She very much wanted to avoid hearing what Graham proposed to pay McGregor.

When Caroline was bathed and tucked in bed, as the voices from the kitchen still went murmuring on, she retreated to her bedroom with a book, rather than go downstairs again and become involved in the negotiations.

At last the voices stopped, and she heard the hollow thud of the back door.

Stiff with cold, she unfolded herself from the bed, where she had curled up, and went down to begin making supper.

Graham was standing in the kitchen, staring out of the window at the retreating figure of McGregor, now barely visible on the drive in the rainy dusk.

"Well," she said, trying to sound casual and friendly, "did you ask him about his wife?"

He turned slowly and looked at her without speaking for a moment, as if she had roused him from a deep abstraction. She could hardly make out his face at all, in the gathering dark, with his back to what light there was.

Then he said, "Oh—yes. It's all fixed up. His wife is going to come along every morning at eight fifteen. Starting on the first. There's a child, too—a girl of six or so. I said she could come, too."

"Oh. Yes, of course. Fine. She and Caroline will be able to play together. It'll be a help, I expect; they'll probably become bosom friends," Jane said with assumed enthusiasm. For some reason her heart sank.

But she switched on the light, opened the hot plate on top of the stove, and fetched out chops and a frying pan. Then she exclaimed, turning and seeing Graham's face properly for the first time, "My dear! Are you all right? You do look tired. You're as white as a sheet."

"Just a bit done up," he muttered. "I think, if you don't mind, I'll have a quick drink and go straight up to bed. I don't feel like any supper." He went into the next room. She heard him clinking in the drinks cupboard, then his dragging step on the stairs.

Jane was very much disconcerted. Graham, an abstemious drinker because of his ulcer, hardly ever resorted to alcohol; hot milk was his standby.

But when she presently took him up a mugful of milk, she found him lying with the light off, a dark, unrelaxed shape under the bedclothes, staring fixedly at the wall. He made no answer when she said, "Graham?" softly; he pretended to be asleep, but she knew he was not.

And when, later, she went up to bed herself, she found the mug of milk still untouched, now covered over with skin, on the bedside table. Graham was silent and motionless, with his eyes shut; but she was fairly sure that he was still awake.

THE NEW ROUTINE STARTED ON ANOTHER WET MONDAY morning.

Mrs. McGregor had sent a message, via her husband, that under no circumstances would she cook. So Jane had spent the previous evening making a steak-and-kidney pie, which merely needed another twenty minutes in the oven, and what she hoped was a sufficient supply of vegetables, fruit jelly, and custard. She hoped that Caroline's constitution would be equal to two months of prefabricated, warmed-over food, and that preparing baby cereal and boiled eggs for Donald did not count as cookery.

Caroline had been troubled and anxious for the past two or three days, unwilling to let her mother out of her sight, reluctant to settle to any pursuit for long, following Jane from room to room. She had reverted to finger-sucking, always a sign with her that she was frightened or unhappy.

Over and over, with painstaking care and thoroughness, Jane had rehearsed and discussed the new program: that she would go off after breakfast in the morning, that she would return every night before bedtime, that kind Mrs. McGregor would be there all day, with her little girl called Susan who would be fun to play with, and that, in any case, this whole affair of Mother's job would last no more than two months—eight weeks—fifty-six days. She made a chart of the

23

days which Caroline could strike off each evening; she promised treats at the weekends; but, she thought dispiritedly, probably all this laborious reassurance only helped to underline the alarming fact that for all of every day, Mother was not going to be there at all. What use were charts and promises? To a child of Caroline's age, two months might as well be forever.

On Monday morning Caroline clung close by Jane uneasily, while she rapidly washed and dried the breakfast dishes, laid out all the prepared food conspicuously, put on makeup and the Mary Quant raincoat which had stood her in good stead for the last four years, and then stared forebodingly up the drive. It would be worse than a nuisance if Mrs. McGregor was going to turn out unreliable.

"Mummy, what's going to *happen* all day when you are gone?"

"Just the same as when I'm at home, precious. You'll play, and go shopping, and do things in the garden if it's fine. Only Mrs. McGregor will be giving you your lunch and taking you for walks instead of me."

Please heaven, don't let Caroline cry at the point of parting.

"And you'll have Susan to play with. Won't that be fun?"

Jane had tried to fix up a meeting between the children beforehand; she had tried several times; but Mrs. McGregor had been away visiting an aunt in Cardiff (for a last fling, her husband conveyed, before going into bondage); then she had had a cold; then little Susan had had a cold. The meeting had failed to materialize.

At last, thank goodness, a pair of figures appeared at the end of the driveway: a woman wheeling a bicycle and a child perched on the carrier.

24

Caroline gripped Jane's hand in a hot, tight clutch.

Reaching the porch at last, Mrs. McGregor unwrapped Susan from about four layers of outer clothing: oilskin, raincoat, coat, cardigan. Jane, holding the door for them to come in, had never seen a child so swaddled; they might have been at Archangel, rather than England in June.

"Hello!" she said, trying to sound cheerful and welcoming. "Isn't this weather terrible? Do come in, quick, where it's dry. Hello, Susan! This is Caroline."

"Good morning, madam," the woman said in a low, repressive tone. She turned, with the massive bundle of outer wear on her arm, carefully propped her bicycle against the porch wall, and at last consented to come through the open door, pushing the wooden-faced Susan before her.

With a shock of chill dismay, Jane realized that Mrs. McGregor's was the face she had noticed staring at her and Tom Roland through the post-office window. That day was several weeks ago now, but she was sure; she would know those pale, watchful eyes anywhere.

They were now—with a sharp, furtive speed like her husband's—taking in all the interior of the house and its furnishings. Feeling more and more uneasy, Jane hurriedly explained where utensils were kept.

"Don't you want to show Susan your toys, darling?" she said to Caroline. But Caroline gripped her hand even tighter, warily eyeing the newcomer, and Susan seemed interested in nothing; she appeared utterly passive and incurious, content to stand still in one spot. But perhaps she was shy, and certainly she was highly disciplined. If she moved even a fraction, Mrs. McGregor snapped, "Susan! This isn't your house! Don't you dare lay a finger on anything!" so fiercely that Jane winced. Susan herself remained impassive.

"Don't worry, honestly, Mrs. McGregor. There's nothing she can hurt. I hope they'll have lots of fun together."

Deeply troubled, nonetheless, Jane stooped with swimming eyes over Donald's cot—but he was fast asleep; she wouldn't wake him—and returned Caroline's tight hug.

"You'll be as good as gold, my precious, won't you?" she whispered. Caroline nodded, looking with curiosity at the unresponsive Susan. Thank goodness, Caroline was going to be sensible, bless her; she wasn't going to cry.

It was the last time, though, that Caroline was sensible; she cried on every subsequent morning at Jane's departure, sometimes having to be forcibly restrained from tearfully following her mother out of the gate and along to the bus stop.

"You'll be sure to be home by six, won't you, madam," said Mrs. McGregor. "There's my husband's supper to get. He works hard all day; he gets very hungry by the evening; and there's Susan's bedtime too. Any later than six wouldn't be at all convenient for me."

"Yes, I do see that. I'm aiming to catch the five-ten train every evening from Cannon Street," Jane promised. "That connects with the half-past-five bus from Culveden station, and will get me home at ten to six. But if the train's late, it sometimes misses the bus—or if I *should* miss the train—you know what offices are; someone always comes in with an urgent inquiry just when you're putting on your coat, and you can't just walk off—"

Mrs. McGregor's expression remained unresponsive; either she did not know what offices were, or she did not choose to.

26

"—you wouldn't mind waiting another ten minutes or so, would you? It wouldn't happen often, I'm sure."

"I couldn't promise to stay after six, madam. McGregor's very particular about having his evening meal on time, and it's going to be late as it is. It wouldn't be convenient for me to stay later."

"But you couldn't just go off and leave the children," Jane said, doing her best to sound calm and reasonable. "This is such an isolated house. It would be different if there were neighbors close at hand."

"I couldn't promise, madam."

For pete's sake, Jane thought, but she did not argue.

THE FOLIA FILMS OFFICE WAS HOUSED IN A NEW SKYSCRAPER block, north of Oxford Street, not far from the British Museum. Jane was officially supposed to be there until five; most of the day's occurrences piled up in the last hour. At ten to five, ignoring the pealing telephone, she threw on her raincoat, grabbed her purse, ran like a deer to the underground station, changed at Holborn, got off at the Bank, and ran even faster around three corners to Cannon Street main line station.

She just managed to get through the platform barrier before it was closed, and threw herself on the five-ten to Culveden, her heart pounding, her mouth dry from swallowing gulps of cold air. If I wanted to lose weight, she thought grimly, a couple of months of this routine would be an excellent way to set about it.

The five-ten was five minutes late arriving at the other end. She had half a minute in which to sprint up the two-hundred-yard sloping station approach, cross a

busy main road, and catch her bus out to South Culveden. She caught it.

When she reached Weir View House, she found Mrs.
McGregor sitting in the kitchen with her coat and hat
on, her eyes fixed on the loudly ticking kitchen clock.
Susan, again swaddled as if for the arctic, was staring
at nothing; a copy of *Home Journal* lay open, un-
regarded, before her. Caroline also was sitting idle, an
unusual state for her. Donald slept in his carry-cot.
Complete silence reigned, except for the clock ticking.

Jane saw at once that the whole place had been
polished to fanatical brightness. Floors, mirrors, windows, furniture, doorknobs, plates, glasses, glittered
as never before. The stove was stoked high and roaring;
the kitchen, tropic hot, smelled of wax polish and
steamy-hot wool.

"Hallo, everybody," Jane said. "How did it go?"

"Quite all right, madam." Mrs. McGregor's tone
was colorless. "We must be off right away. Come on,
Susan. Hurry up. Don't dawdle now! Father will be
waiting."

"Had a nice day, my precious? Had fun, Susan?"

Susan made no answer.

Caroline looked up and answered, almost inaudibly,
"It was very nice."

She did not run to hug her mother. She stood against
the wall, her hands by her sides.

Jane saw the McGregors off, and then put Caroline to
bed, taking pains to be extra loving, carrying her up the
stairs, prolonging the bath games, sitting on her bed for
a chat.

"What did you do, darling, all day?" she asked.

"It was very nice," Caroline said.

"What happened? Did you enjoy playing with
Susan? Did you talk to each other?"

28

"She's very nice."

"What games did you play?" Jane persisted, hoping to penetrate beyond this blank.

"We didn't play games. She looked at my toys and I watched her."

"I expect you'll think of more things to do tomorrow."

Jane felt reluctant to probe any further, but she was profoundly troubled by Caroline's unaccustomed quietness and apathy.

She mentioned it to Graham when he got home.

"Oh, it's nothing. Don't bother your head about it," he said rather impatiently. "It's just the new routine. You'll see. She'll be chattering like a starling in a couple of days."

But he spoke as if his mind were only half on what he was saying. He was glancing about the obsessively clean kitchen. "Christ, Mrs. McGregor has got the place spruced up, hasn't she? Even red ocher on the porch bricks. Shown you up a bit, my dear."

"I don't like red ocher," Jane said temperately. "I prefer the natural color of the bricks. I specifically told her not to worry about housework, that I'd do the essentials on the weekends. We're in the country; the house can't get too grubby in a couple of months. I'd rather she took the children for walks. They've not been out all day. Graham, do you think you could arrange to be home by six each evening while I'm doing this job at Folia? Mrs. McGregor insists she must get off on the dot, and I'm scared stiff of missing the train one night; it was an awfully close thing this evening. She's being a bit unbendable about it. She says she won't wait if I don't get back."

"Well, that's not unreasonable of her," he said. "After all, she's got her own chores to do at home, on top of ours. You can't expect her to wait till all hours. It's a long day for her as it is.''

"I know that, but—''

"Anyway, *I* can't possibly get home, I'm afraid. That time between five and seven is absolutely crucial for seeing clients in a social way, getting to know their likes and dislikes. My coming back is out of the question. But, damn it, surely you can manage? After all, you're doing Folia a favor, going back like this—they asked you. The least they can do is arrange for you to get off when you want.''

"Unfortunately,'' said Jane, "just as with you, around five is the busiest time there. Film people don't seem to start functioning before about 3 P.M.''

He shrugged. "Well, it just can't be helped. Anyway, is it such a life-and-death matter if the kids are left alone for fifteen minutes?''

Jane stared at him incredulously.

"You often go down to the post office or the grocer's leaving Donald here asleep,'' he pointed out. "If you remember, I said only last week that you'd probably have the N.S.P.C.C. blowing down your neck.''

"That's a bit different, Graham. I'm only five minutes' run away then. I know I can get back fast. But to leave Donald *and* Caroline—she's four; she'd be scared to death all on her own in the house at that time of day. And suppose I was held up, suppose there was a derailment or something, and I *couldn't* get home?''

"Oh, what rubbish. How often are there derailments, I ask you? Anyway,'' said Graham irritably. "whatever happens, we mustn't upset the McGregors. Do you understand? They are—they could be immensely useful to us. We simply can't afford to put their backs up. Culveden isn't crawling with couples prepared to do the double job the way they are. You've just got to be sure of getting home on time—that's all there is to it.''

''I don't think I really like Mrs. McGregor,'' Jane said doubtfully. ''I think I'll ask Miss Ames if she can't think of someone else who wouldn't be such a stickler for getting away on the dot. After all, it doesn't have to be McGregor's wife. Someone who wasn't so obsessed about her husband's supper would be much more satisfactory.''

''You're being utterly unreasonable,'' Graham exploded. ''For all I know, McGregor wouldn't want to stay on if his wife didn't come, too. Just because you've taken one of your stupid, irrational prejudices against the woman—after *one day,* for god's sake! It's just prejudice. Nothing to do with the time thing at all, if you ask me.''

''Well—in a way—yes. I'm worried about Caroline.''

''After ten hours! Honestly! You must be off your head.'' He glanced at his watch. ''Lord, I must go. I promised to meet Tom Roland at the pub.''

In the doorway he paused. ''I meant that, you know, Jane. We must *not* upset these McGregors. You want this operation to go smoothly, don't you? Well, then, keep them happy. Did you remember to lay in something for tomorrow's midday meal?''

''Yes,'' said Jane tiredly. ''I got some meat at the delicatessen in Southampton Row. I only hope Susan can eat it.''

Susan, apparently, had not fancied the steak-and-kidney pie.

When Graham had gone, Jane tackled the washing, which Mrs. McGregor apparently did not consider to be part of her duties. There was an unusual quantity of it; much of her time must have been spent in changing the children out of one lot of clothes and into another.

Then Jane peeled and scrubbed vegetables, and made

31

a pudding. Then she went up to have a last look at Caroline. The child was in a deep sleep, very much flushed; but as she slept, she moved restlessly, muttering and turning from side to side.

Leaning close, Jane caught the words she was saying over and over: "It was very nice. It was very nice. It was very nice. . . ."

THREE NIGHTS LATER, JANE DID MISS THE BUS HOME FROM the station. A thick summer fog had settled down at five, and her train was twelve minutes late. She tried in vain for a taxi—taxis were scarce as white blackberries outside Culveden station at any time, and the few there this evening were instantly snapped up by large, athletic, golf-playing stockbrokers, one of whom knocked Jane sprawling with his briefcase and umbrella as he nipped ahead of her.

By running like a maniac down two blocks and across the corner of the common, she was able to catch a different bus, which deposited her within a twelve-minute walk of home—a six-minute run. Unfortunately, after her various different sprints, her legs were so weak that they felt like discarded banana peel; by the time she reached her own driveway, she had slowed down to a kind of scouts' amble.

As she hobbled up the drive to the house, she noticed that Donald's carry-cot was out on the porch. Hitherto she had been unsuccessful in her attempts to persuade Mrs. McGregor to leave him out in the fresh air; each night when she arrived home the cot was invariably in the stifling hot kitchen, with the stove roaring and every window shut.

She thrust open the front door, having hastily surveyed the cot to make sure Donald was all right—yes, sleeping peacefully—and ran in.

Caroline was sitting alone in the kitchen. She had found some of Graham's sketching charcoal—how had she managed to get hold of that? Surely he always kept it locked up in his old-fashioned rolltop desk?—and on his best three-by-four sheets of cartridge paper she was drawing immense lions and tigers. Her face and hands were black with charcoal dust; broken sticks lay scattered around and trodden into the tiles; the thin blue muslin party dress she had on was also smothered in black grit. Jane hoped that it would wash out, but had little confidence.

"Where's Mrs. McGregor, my precious? And Susan?"

"Don't know," said Caroline. "They went out."

"When?"

Caroline looked vague. "Some time," she said.

Time meant little to her.

Now Jane recalled that there had been no bicycle on the porch. They must have gone home. Mrs. McGregor must have carried out her threat and departed without waiting for Jane's return.

Jane raged silently. She used all the wicked words she knew, in her mind, pacing about the insultingly polished kitchen. Mrs. McGregor must have known it was the fog—thick, here—that had delayed her, that she couldn't help it, and yet the woman hadn't had the common decency to wait fifteen minutes. . . .

"Come along, then, up to bed, my lamb. Let's get you out of this dusty dress. I'll just fetch in Donald. You start up the stairs."

They were in the bathroom getting Caroline unbuttoned when a sound from below stopped Jane short. She darted out on to the landing and, looking over the

33

banisters, saw Mrs. McGregor with Susan down by the front door. The two pale, expressionless faces, beaded with drops of mist, looked up at her.

"You're back then, madam?"

"The train crawled all the way from Cannon Street because of the fog," Jane said. "It missed the bus. I'm sorry I was late—it couldn't be helped. I thought you'd already gone."

"Just hanging out some clothes on the line," Mrs. McGregor said blandly.

With Susan? In the foggy dark? For fifteen minutes? And where was her bicycle?

"I'll be off then, madam."

In the pale eyes there showed, for a fleeting moment, something savagely vindictive. Perhaps that's taught you a lesson, my lady? You'll be a bit nippier next time?

Then Mrs. McGregor took her bicycle from where it stood concealed, around a corner out of sight, mounted Susan on the carrier, and rode off.

"Why have you got your best blue dress on, honey?" said Jane, when she had taken a few deep breaths and gone back to the bathroom.

"Some people came to tea."

"Oh, who?"

Caroline looked nonplussed. "Don't know."

"Friends of Mrs. McGregor?"

"S'pose so."

Well, after all, why shouldn't she? There was no harm in that, Jane thought wearily, going downstairs. She noticed that a set of glass teaplates, a wedding-present set that she hardly ever used, had been taken out and left on the kitchen dresser; so had her grand-mother's silver teapot and a pretty old slipware dish that was actually quite valuable. But the things had been washed up and were not hurt. And the fact that

34

they had been left out in conspicuous positions seemed to show that Mrs. McGregor did not intend to make a secret of her having had friends in. Why should she? She had a right to see her friends and certainly at present, tethered as she was at Weir View House between eight and six, her only chance was to see them here.

Stifling what she told herself was perfectly irrational resentment at having her new house used for entertaining strangers, Jane started making a lamb stew, which Mrs. McGregor could heat up for lunch next day, and a sponge pudding. Susan was known to be fond of jam sponge.

A week later, one evening, as Jane raced up the Culveden station approach for her bus, she became aware of a Rover, which had just pulled out of the station parking lot, slowing down ahead of her.

Tom Roland's head came out of the car window, and he said, "They still don't allow women to enter the Grand National, so your hopes are in vain. And I've heard the Olympics are a terrible racket. Do you want a lift home, by any chance?"

"Oh, Tom, yes! Bless you." Jane forgot her resolution to call him Mr. Roland.

"Where have you been these last weeks?" he asked, whooshing his car over the railway bridge with a soaring sensation of flight.

Jane cast a triumphant glance back at the hated bus, now just slowing down to the stop. "I've been working in town—went back to my old job for a temporary spell."

"With Folia? So that's why I never seen you about the village anymore. Are you enjoying it?"

"Not an awful lot, really. Oh, it's lovely seeing the people I knew there again. But, you know how it is, lots of the ones who were there when I was have left now, and anyway—"

Somehow, without meaning to do so, she found herself telling Tom about all her problems with Mrs. McGregor and getting home on time.

"But what a frightful woman she sounds!" he said. "I never did like her face, but I didn't realize she was such a hag. Can't you tell her to go to hell? Surely the job's not worth all this agony?"

"It mightn't be easy to get anyone else right away. And we really do need the money. The house cost a lot more than we reckoned it was going to. You know how houses are."

Tom looked thoughtful. "How much longer does the job go on?"

"Oh, another four weeks. It's not too bad really. And Mrs. McGregor's perfectly efficient in other ways."

"McGregor's wife? I always did think the Welsh were a peculiar race," Tom said irrelevantly.

"Almost as bad as the Scots," Jane agreed, laughing. "Though my husband's one of those, so I shouldn't say that."

"True-blue British myself—apart from the French and Irish strains, of course."

After that, Jane noticed that more often than not, Tom was on her train of an evening and would pick her up in the station approach, or greet her at Cannon Street. It was astonishing the way he could pick her out of the throng of commuters rushing for their various homebound trains. Then they would travel down together, chattering about their respective jobs. Tom, it seemed, was doing research for a new television series on Beds Through the Ages, which entailed constant visits to museums and libraries, and script conferences at Toledo House. Whether his presence on the train was a complete coincidence each time, Jane preferred to leave in the realm beyond speculation; she was just unfeignedly glad to be driven home night after night. The blessed respite of the short ride from the station, instead of her desperate gallop for the bus, not to mention Tom's easy, cheerful chat, made her able to bear with more fortitude Mrs. McGregor's daily installment of martyrdom.

"Was the stew all right, Mrs. McGregor?"

"Miss Caroline ate some, madam. Susan and I can't digest veal."

"Oh, dear," said Jane. "Why didn't you tell me when I suggested it? I could just as easily have got something else."

Jane spent her short lunch periods (since she was obliged to leave early in the evening, her tender conscience and the press of work rarely allowed her to take more than half an hour at midday) feverishly ransacking the rather scanty but exotic provision shops in the neighborhood of her office for comestibles that would be acceptable to Mrs. McGregor and Susan. Susan appeared to enjoy nothing but frozen potato chips; Mrs. McGregor suffered from a disability that she referred to as gastric stomach; this prevented her from eating anything fibrous, rich, strongly flavored, acid, alkali, or foreign. Fish, eggs, ham, beef, liver (which Jane's children loved), onions, cheese, nearly all vegetables, and pastry came under these categories.

"I had some bread and tea," said Mrs. McGregor, sniffing in a virtuous and put-upon manner. "It didn't matter...."

"I hope you managed to get out for a walk this lovely sunny day?"

"Oh, I couldn't, madam. Wouldn't have dared to. With all this grass around about, my hay fever. . . .

"The catch on the back door's not reliable, madam.

37

Anybody could get in while I'm upstairs, seeing to the children. . . .

"The coal never came, madam. There won't be enough to last over the weekend now. I didn't know if you'd want me to do anything about it. . . ."

"Oh, I wish you'd rung the order office. Could you possibly do that tomorrow?" Jane said, wondering why this simple course of action had not occurred to Mrs. McGregor. "It's easier for you to do it from here than for me to do it from London."

"I didn't know if you'd want me to, madam. . . ."

"The lavatory plug doesn't seem to be working, madam. I didn't send for anybody—didn't know if you'd want me to. . . .

"That cat's bitten me, madam. In my opinion it's not safe to be around with children in the house. It's not like an ordinary cat. It's vicious, more like a wild animal. In my opinion it ought to be put away. I make sure it doesn't come anywhere near my Susan."

In fact several times Jane had come home to find Plum, the most gentle and unaggressive Siamese in the world, shut up in her bedroom, where, bored with incarceration, he had knocked over eau-de-cologne bottles and sharpened his claws on the basketwork couch. Jane prayed that Graham would not notice.

"No, I couldn't go for a walk today, madam. The sun was so bright it made my eyes irritate. And my ankles have been bad again. Susan isn't feeling quite the thing, either. I think those foreign biscuits didn't agree with her. The baby's eyes looked puffy." (Mrs. McGregor always called him the baby, never Donald.) "Anyway, I was afraid of the laundry coming while we were out."

Only once a week could Jane be sure of the children's getting some exercise and fresh air—on the day when she left a written order for the grocer. Then Mrs. Mc-

38

Gregor would sally valiantly out, rain or shine, her little button mouth pursed with resolution. Several times the children had been drenched when she had felt obliged to take them through heavy rain. Once, according to her mother, Susan had caught a cold verging on pneumonia from the wild winds outside the grocer's store; but still, fall who might by the wayside, the order must go through.

"If it's wet," suggested Jane, hoping to ease matters, "why don't you phone the list? Mr. Rolf wouldn't mind?"

Mrs. McGregor looked negative but said nothing.

One day Jane herself, having forgotten the list until after she had left, composed it on the train and phoned home from her office.

She heard the telephone ring about thirty times, until she would have been ready to believe there was no one in the house if it had not been so early in the morning: Donald's bath and feed time. At last, Mrs. McGregor's voice—surly, suspicious—said,

"Hello. What is it? Who's that?"

"Oh, Mrs. McGregor—it's Mrs. Drummond here. I forgot to give you the grocery-store list, and they deliver tomorrow. If you've got a moment to spare I'll give it to you now. There's a pencil and memo pad by the phone, or ought to be."

An immensely long pause followed. Jane thought she heard breathing.

"Hello?" she said puzzled. "Are you still there? Can you see the pencil?"

She heard a clink. Apparently Mrs. McGregor had laid down the receiver. A moment later Jane heard her calling Caroline. Then, shortly after, came her whisper, evidently not intended for Jane's ears, but audible nonetheless:

39

"Come here. Write down what I say. Never mind that, now. Write what I tell you."

She's making *Caroline* do it? thought Jane baffled. Why? All things considered, Caroline wrote and spelled amazingly for a four-year-old with a passionate desire to read books, but still—?

"Are you ready?" Jane asked, hearing the receiver click again.

"Yes, madam."

"I do wish you didn't feel it necessary to call me madam," Jane suddenly exclaimed. "I'd so much rather you called me Mrs. Drummond. Couldn't you?"

Silence.

"Oh, well. . . . A pound of rice," Jane said, sighing.

"Pound of rice," echoed Mrs. McGregor.

"Two dozen eggs . . . cornflakes . . . spaghetti . . ."

Mrs. McGregor's voice echoed each item; then there would be a long pause; then she would say, "Yes, madam?"

Next day—Saturday—Jane was at home when the order was delivered. Sure enough, there in the box with all the goods was a bit of paper with the list written out in Caroline's toppling script and eccentric spelling.

"Why did Mrs. McGregor get you to write the list, darling?"

"Don't know."

Caroline was becoming more and more dour and monosyllabic. She seemed unable or unwilling to answer questions, but haunted her mother, never more than a couple of feet away, all the time that Jane was at home. Although dry at night without effort or training since the age of eighteen months, she had now begun wetting her bed again, so Jane had sheets to wash in the evenings as well as Donald's things. Caroline was bitterly

ashamed of this, though Jane never dreamed of re-
proaching her.

"Those are my sheets, aren't they? I wetted my bed,
didn't I?" she said, watching one evening as Jane hung
them out to dry. For a wonder, it was not raining.

"Don't worry about it, darling. Who cares? I don't
mind. Come on—up the stairs to bed."

But Caroline reverted to the subject after her bath.
"Why do I wet my bed, Mummy?"

What to say? Because you are under strain, because
we are all under strain? Say something about Mrs.
McGregor? Ask something? Suggest a connection?
Better not.

To Caroline's expectant and anxious look, Jane answered, hugging her, "Probably because there's such
a lot of rain at night, and you hear it going pitter-
patter on the roof. Now snuggle into bed with Pinky."

Pinky was Caroline's old comfort-blanket which she
had taken to using again, cuddling it against her cheek
and sucking her finger whenever she was not doing
something with her hands. Pinky by now was so old,
moulting, and tattered that Jane had prudently cut it in
half and stowed one half away in her wardrobe drawer,
just in case the other half disintegrated entirely before
the need for it was past.

"Anyway," she said, "it was very clever of you to
write the grocery list. That was a very grown-up thing
to do. Wasn't Mrs. McGregor pleased?"

"Don't know."

A wild conjecture crossed Jane's mind. Was Mrs.
McGregor not able to read or write? Was she dyslectic
or retarded? Certainly Susan might be; she showed
definite signs of backwardness in her lethargic move-
ments, slow reactions, and lack of concentration. Jane
had abandoned any hope of the children's being satis-

41

factory playmates. Now she tried to remember if she had ever seen Mrs. McGregor actually reading; turning the pages of magazines, yes; looking at the pictures, as hatted, coated, scarved, and swaddled, she and Susan waited for Jane's return. But never actually reading.

What must it be like to live in the present-day world and not be able to read? Surely the whole of your surroundings must seem in some sinister way leagued against you.

I ought to tackle her about it, Jane thought. If it's really so, it probably accounts for—accounts for a lot of the way she behaves. And she ought to have help for it.

But faced with the unspoken, unmistakable hostility in Mrs. McGregor's eyes, imagining McGregor's deadly affront—no less for being veiled in assumed deference —at such a piece of condescension, Jane quailed. She could not bring herself to raise any more than the basic, essential points that kept the arrangement just ticking along.

Of late, McGregor had taken to coming and sitting in the kitchen with his wife, and escorting her home as soon as Jane arrived. Myfanwy McGregor was an object of vague, unformulated dislike and distrust to Jane; Tim, she definitely knew that she hated and feared. She could hardly have said why though. His manner was perfectly respectful, verging on the servile, but there was something behind the surface manner, something wily and powerful and aware, which gave her the cold grue. It seemed as if he knew shameful secrets about her which she did not know herself. When at night she came home into the hot, stuffy, brightly lit kitchen with its smell of recklessly applied furniture polish and dirty old commando beret, she instantly felt the alien, unwelcoming atmosphere; it was like forcing her way into the den of a pair of wild beasts.

The evenings were too short to abolish the Mc-
Gregors' atmosphere in the house; even when she rolled
into bed, dog-tired, she could still fell it all about her.
It was as if they were gradually taking over psychic
occupation, and had left their elemental presences behind them to keep guard, watching and despising.

Off in the morning, leaving Caroline in tears, sometimes struggling against Mrs. McGregor's grip, sometimes sodden and apathetic; back at night, feeling like
an interloper under her own roof: Jane found her days
beginning to take on a nightmare pattern of similarity,
each end caught in a trap.

She dreamed every night of trains. Dragonlike ex-
presses raced away from her as she toiled hopelessly
after them on flabby, exhausted legs, and Mrs. Mc-
Gregor smirked in triumph from a high window, saying,
"I don't know where the children are, madam. They got
out several stations back. I daresay they're down playing by the weir."

McGregor had not yet mended the fences between the
garden and the weir, though repeatedly asked to do so
by Jane. He listened to her requests with an insulting
air of having better things to do than carry out fiddling
jobs at the request of a fussing woman. He and Graham
were busy turning the front stretch of land into something suitable for a show house, with exquisitely turfed
banks and planted shrubs and flagged paths and what
was going to be a lily pond. At least, presumably the
orders came from Graham; he was hardly seen at home
just now; the housing project in Hastings occupied him
early and late.

When he did stop to take notice of Jane, he said
rather irritably, "You're getting very thin. I should
have thought going back to work would have done you
good, women's lib and all that. You said often enough
you'd like to go back. What's up? Job not going right?"

"Oh, it's all right," Jane said moderately. "Just a bit tiring. That's all."

"The whole setup seems to be working so well, I think you should consider going on with it permanently," Graham said with a slightly overdone air of having just hit on this notion. "It's much better for you really—gives you an interest outside the home. And the kids are okay—Donald looks pink and sturdy enough, bless him."

They were standing by Donald's cot. Graham, who, Jane thought, completely loved only this one creature outside himself, always made a point of going up to look at his son when he arrived home, however late.

"Donald's fine," she agreed. "But I'm not a bit happy about Caroline."

"Oh, she'll be all right in a little. Girls always miss their mothers more. She's just going through a sulky phase. She'll get over it."

It was at this moment that Jane, to her own incredulity, found herself calmly considering the apparently irrelevant notion of divorce. *Divorce?* Divorce *Graham?*

But then Caroline called from the bathroom, "I'm dried, Mummy. Can I have a story in bed—just one?"

As soon as Jane settled on the bed, Caroline gripped her hand. Feeling the small, tight clutch, Jane thought, Take her away from what is at least a home? Make her leave these familiar surroundings, make her move yet again? (For there was no question, if it came to a breach, who would move out. Graham would certainly want to stay here; while, left on her own, Jane would not wish to stay in the heavily mortgaged Weir View House for a month—no, not for a week.)

Then, also, there was the consideration that divorce would mean separating Caroline not only from her father (who, indeed, hardly noticed her existence) but from her young brother, whom she devotedly loved. Graham would have fought legal authorities all the way to the House of Lords for the right to keep his baby son. Jane was sure in her bones of that; the thought of the struggle made her wilt even before she had fully formed it.

No, best keep the home together for the time, and make at least the semblance of a happy place for the children to grow in, until they were old enough to notice that it was not; then would be the time to reconsider.

Graham returned to the subject of her job at supper.

"Yes," he remarked, thoughtfully cutting himself a slice of ham, "now you've got back into harness again, I think you ought to reckon to stay on with Folia permanently. After all, they like you. You're good at the job—"

Jane had a foreboding qualm but was able to reply, "They won't need me any more soon. Wilshaw is out of hospital and will be back on schedule."

She was relieved when Graham, without forcing the issue or, in fact, appearing to notice her reply, went on casually, "Oh, by the way, could you get them to let you have all your money in a lump now? I'd very much like to pay old Tom for that machine."

"Yes—all right," she said doubtfully. "I suppose they won't mind. But haven't you any money in your account?"

"I'll have some on Monday," he said quickly, "but I'd like to settle with Tom as soon as possible. After all, he *is* an old friend."

She let this go by and, against her own inclination, agreed to ask for advance payment.

45

CAROLINE'S BIRTHDAY HAPPENED TO FALL IN THE MIDDLE of the following week. Jane, having passed over all her Folia money to Graham, asked him if he could let her have a bit for housekeeping.

"Surely you don't need housekeeping money when you're earning?" he said, astonished and vexed.

"But I just gave you—"

"Look, I can't stay arguing now. I've got to be in Hastings by ten. In any case, I haven't any spare cash right now."

"A check would be all right. It's Caroline's birthday tomorrow, and I'm spending such a lot on food that I haven't anything over to buy her a present—"

"Oh, for heaven's sake! Get her something at Woolworth's! What's the difference to a four-year-old? She probably doesn't even know it's her birthday—"

He was gone, striding through the rain to the garage.

Jane just had time, after Mrs. McGregor came, and before her bus, to dart up to her bedroom and rummage out the only good ornament she possessed: a pale-green jade Chinese medallion with a good-luck ideograph in gold, and a dangling gold dragon beneath; the whole thing slung on a gold chain so fine that she hardly ever found the courage to wear it in case it broke. But she loved looking at it in its little tortoiseshell box; it had been left to her by her mother who had died when Jane was eight.

On the bus she thought some more about divorce;

46

once lodged in her mind, the idea was hard to expel. But two parents must be better than one, she thought; and even if Graham is a bit feckless about money, I daresay I can make up for it by being careful. And he'll get to take more notice of Caroline by and by. Being brought up by one parent alone is so very scaring (she remembered the long desperate times of acute anxiety when her father, an archaeologist, had been away on various digs) that almost any security, however tenuous, must surely be better.

Probably if I hadn't had all those anxieties in childhood, I'd have thought a bit more carefully, waited a bit longer, before marrying Graham.

The bus arrived at Culveden station before she had time to face or dodge the concomitant thought: And then I mightn't have married him at all. Which might have been a good thing?

Selling the jade pendant proved more difficult than she had expected. Several places said they weren't interested in antique jewelry, or offered ridiculously low sums. Her father had told her that it was worth quite a lot of money, but a man in a shop near the British Museum, the likeliest place, said he couldn't offer more than seven pounds fifty for it; at Jane's faint sound of dismay he grudgingly raised this amount to nine pounds. There wasn't, he told her, any demand for this kind of ornament at present. Jane was surprised, as his shop seemed full of similar things— though not so beautiful. But time was flying; she could not afford to stand arguing; she had to sell it. And the nine pounds provided enough to buy a very handsome large woolly bear for Caroline, and a cheerful red and green and white striped sweater. Feeling that it would be embarrassing if Caroline had presents and the other child nothing, Jane bought a matching sweater for

Susan as well. Then, having already overrun the usual time she allotted herself for her lunch hour, she hastily laid in a preroasted chicken for tomorrow's lunch, at the delicatessen; expensive, but at least everyone would eat chicken.

Caroline loved the bear. Jane, watching her face of radiant delight as she carried him around the house and showed him the view from various windows, felt the sale of the medallion had been worth it; that, if nothing else, was an unqualified success. But Mrs. McGregor plainly though less than nothing of the striped sweaters. Too late, Jane recalled that Susan never wore knitted things over her frilly dresses, unless they were fluffy angora cardigans in pastel colors; she possessed none of this kind of tough, bright gear. A hope that matching clothes might formulate a bond between the two children quickly dwindled and died; it seemed unlikely that Susan would ever get to wear her sweater. Caroline, prancing about in hers over a pair of brown corduroy pants, hugging her bear, seemed a reasonable image of her sometime cheerful self.

Mrs. McGregor, coldly and briskly bundling the other sweater into the capacious brown rexine shopping bag that accompanied her everywhere, said, "I daresay there'll be tears later. We'll have to see the birthday girl doesn't get overexcited. All these presents—"

"Oh, there's nothing else," Jane said swiftly. "That's the lot. She'll soon simmer down. I hoped if she had a bear she might not cling quite so much to her old pink blanket"; and escaped before Caroline's happiness could diminish.

THAT EVENING, WHEN JANE ARRIVED BREATHLESS AND GASP-
ing at Cannon Street station, she found it cordoned off
by police. A huge, impatient crowd swayed to and fro
in the street outside and in the station yard, rapidly
increasing every instant as more and more would-be
travelers piled up on its fringes.

"What is it? What's happened?" Jane asked a burly,
bowler-hatted man beside her.

"I don't know," said he, furiously shoving. "All I
know is, I shall miss the five eight to Maidstone. Let
us through, can't you? Why can't you let us through?"

Police loudspeaker vans began to nose through the
is said to have been deposited in the Left-Luggage de-
crowd, broadcasting a warning: "A parcel of explosive
partment. As soon as it is cleared, normal train de-
partures will be resumed. Until then, we ask you please
to be patient, and if possible, take alternative services
from other main-line terminals."

But no other main-line terminals served Culveden.

"These damn silly acts of protest!" the bowler-
hatted man burst out, red-faced. "Call themselves the
Justice Brigade, or some bloody childish fancy name
like that, cause a lot of trouble and inconvenience to
people who never did them any harm, that they never
even *met*—justice indeed! I'd justice 'em. I'd string
'em all up, I tell you! What this country wants is the
birch rod and capital punishment brought back. And
then, when they've taken about seven hours searching

49

the cloakrooms, they'll find there was nothing there at all—"

Seven hours! Jane's heart fell horribly. She looked at her watch. Half past five already! She must ring home *at once,* and explain what had happened. Would Mrs. McGregor be reasonable about it this time? What would she say?

Of course there was an immense queue waiting at the nearest phone booth; it seemed to be the only one in working order in the whole city of London. Jane worked her way slowly to the head of the procession and took her turn in the booth.

She put back the receiver and stood staring as if in shock. A woman angrily rapping with a two-penny piece on the glass door recalled her, and she stepped out of the booth mechanically, while the woman shoved past her and let the heavy door swing shut.

Who could she turn to for help? Who could she call? In her ears she could still hear the cold triumphant ring of Mrs. McGregor's voice. She might have been waiting for this occasion all her life.

"No, I'm sorry, madam. My husband has friends coming this evening. It *wouldn't* be possible for me to stay. I can't wait a minute after six—it's quite out of the question. No, I certainly couldn't take the children with me. How could I get them all home? Besides, it wouldn't be convenient, not with company coming. . . ."

The woman had come out of the phone booth. An old man was in there now, slowly reading the instructions. Jane took her place in the queue again and worked up to the front. She rang Graham's office and got his secretary.

"May I speak to Mr. Drummond? . . . His wife."

He must, he just must manage to get home. Just for

once he could arrange it; with the car he could just about do it in time.

"I'm sorry, Mr. Drummond has been at Hastings all day. He said he would not be returning to the office this evening. Number in Hastings you could phone? Oh, no, I'm afraid not, Mrs. Drummond. He's probably out on the building site."

Or at some plushy seaside pub, Jane thought, conducting research into the social likes and dislikes of his clients.

Blankly she stared at the black bakelite receiver. What now? Who? What could she do? Who could she ring? Miss Ames was away on a fortnight's holiday. The police at Culveden? It would hardly make for good relations with the McGregors—or with Graham—but they seemed the only resource. She fumbled for more coins, found she had none, and started frantically edging her way through the crowd towards a tobacconist's kiosk.

"Janey! There you are! I've been searching the whole station for you."

His voice was as welcome to her ears as the sound of the five-ten would have been, chugging in to its appointed platform.

"*Tom!* Oh, Tom, I'm in such a fix. Do advise me."

She poured out her tale, unashamedly dabbing the tears of desperate anxiety from her eyes.

"And they'll be alone in the house *now,* don't you see? That—that bloody woman will have gone off and left them. And I'm so hungry and tired my mind's not functioning terribly well—I simply can't think what to *do,* short of h-hiring a helicopter—"

"My dear, that woman! What a hundred-watt bitch. But don't worry another second. I've got Peter Anstey putting up at my house; he's there now; we're col-

51

laborating on this Tale of a Four-Poster thing. I'll call him right away and tell him to go across and sit with them. He's a confirmed old B.B.C. bloke—that's an absolute guarantee of respectability and goodheartedness. He'll look after them like that she-wolf, you know the one I mean—"

All the time he spoke he was skillfully edging his way to the phone booth, and now, with a winning smile at the man who had just reached the front of the queue, he slid gently past and entered the booth.

Jane heard gratified murmurs of "Did you see who that was?" "Wasn't it Tom Roland?" "Yes, I'm sure it was!"

No one, apparently, minded being made to wait for their turn by a TV celebrity. It was a hopelessly unfair world, Jane felt weakly. She watched Tom hold two short, animated conversations.

"That's fixed then," he said, emerging. "And I've arranged for a hired car to pick us up here in ten minutes, if we can fight our way back to the street again. I should think we just have time for a short drink on the way, and then we ought to synchronize nicely."

But Jane said if he didn't mind she would sooner settle for a sandwich.

THE MOMENT AFTER SHE FOUND HERSELF IN THE ENORMOUS, lavish chauffeur-driven car, sitting on smooth gray upholstery, whirling silently homeward, she fell fast asleep, leaning against Tom's shoulder, holding the roses Tom had bought her.

"I—I'm sorry, Tom. I simply can't keep awake."
The relief from worry was so great.

"Don't trouble your head," he said. "I take it kindly
—as a mark of confidence."

Jane had already fallen asleep; he was talking to
himself.

Her sleep was deep, but of short duration. At Brom-
ley she woke and wondered for an instant where she
could be, why she had this unusual feeling of re-
laxation. Whose arm could be around her? Not
Graham's?

"Don't start like a frighted fawn, "Tom said. "It's
impossible to sleep comfortably in a car without sup-
port. Go back to sleep again; we aren't there yet."

"No, I'm awake now. I feel fine." She sat up straight.

"You're overdoing it," Tom said chidingly. "All
this dashing for trains and buses."

"It's fun though." Jane gave him a wan smile.

"Isn't Graham at all worried about you? You're as
thin as a knitting needle."

"Graham's got enough to worry about. He's so busy
himself."

"Where did you two meet?" Tom asked irrelevantly.

"In Malta. He was out there working full-time as
architect for a big firm of contractors putting up holiday flats."

"And what were you doing?"

"Looking after my father. We lived there—we'd
moved out there when I was small because the climate
was better for my mother's lungs. And then, when
she died, we stayed because Malta was a handy jump-
ing-off place for my father's expeditions—he was an
archaeologist."

"Would I know his name?"

"Julius Dillon."

53

"Professor Dillon. Good God, I should hope so. He died seven or eight years ago. Am I right?"

"Yes. He was ill for a couple of years first."

"And you met Graham there and married him?"

"Yes."

"You've had quite a tough time, haven't you?"

"Oh, good heavens, no." Jane was shocked. "So then Graham and I came back to England, when his job there finished, and I started working at Folia."

"And that was where I met you." Changing the subject, Tom began to tell a long, ludicrous, and random-seeming tale about how the Culveden Borough Council were attempting to prosecute him for installing a second lavatory without planning permission, although he had three times pointed out that his house contained two already and that the one in question was being installed by his next-door neighbor.

"The minds of local government officials are like unprogrammed computers. By the way, talking of drains"—he broke off to say, "McGregor—a man I very much mistrust and wouldn't employ if he didn't have such a talent for keeping my horribly unreliable drains just chugging along—tells me that the Hovermow is giving a lot of trouble. It hovers all lopsided, apparently."

"Does it? I didn't know—"

"So will you tell Graham that I'm reducing the price by fifty quid? In fact, I'll take the damned thing back altogether if you like—I hate to think I've sold you a pup—so he needn't worry about paying me at all. Just tell McGregor to stick it back in my shed."

"Graham hasn't paid you already?" Jane said blankly. "But I was sure—"

"I was in no hurry," Tom said swiftly. "I'd told him any time would do. Tell him to get McGregor to trundle it back. A useless mower is worse than none."

Jane's mind was a turmoil of new worry. It was a week since she had handed over her Folia money to Graham. Why hadn't he paid Tom yet? He couldn't have forgotten. They had met several times at the pub according to his breakfast-table reports. And Graham certainly didn't seem to have any money anymore.

So what had he done with it?

WHEN THEY REACHED WEIR VIEW HOUSE, ALL WAS PEACE-ful. Donald slept in his cot in the porch. In the green-walled sitting room Peter Anstey, a television actor and director of considerable renown, was giving a full-cast performance of Goldilocks and the Three Bears, taking all the parts in turn, and keeping Caroline in blissful fits of laughter. Glasses of beer and orange squash stood companionably on the coffee table, but neither had been touched; actor and audience were far too absorbed.

Jane thought with a pang what a long time it was since she had heard Caroline laugh like that.

"Mummy! *Mummy!* Listen to Peter doing Father Bear."

Caroline flew to her mother and hugged her, then rushed back and tugged Peter's hand. "Again! Do it again!"

Peter—who himself looked, in fact, not at all unlike some lovable furry animal, round and pink with dust-colored hair and gold-rimmed glasses—obliged in a voice that sounded as if it came up from under the floor-boards: "How do you do, Mrs. Drummond?"

"Oh, you are an angel!" Jane said with heartfelt sincerity. "I just don't know how to begin to thank you."

"It's been just great," Peter, who was evidently Canadian, assured her with equal sincerity. "We've had a ball."

"I hope Caroline's been hospitable."

"She was properly suspicious at first; but luckily I got here just before your domestic help left, and we'd met the children in the street when I was out strolling with Tom one afternoon, so all was well."

"Oh, so Mrs. McGregor knows you're here."

Perhaps she wouldn't really have left the children on their own, Jane thought; perhaps I've been misjudging her.

She went to the kitchen to put the dark red roses Tom had bought her into a vase, and fetch another couple of glasses. What would Graham think, she wondered, if he arrived home and found Tom and Peter under his roof? Enchanted, no doubt.

But Graham did not come home, and Tom, when he had downed his drink rather fast, said, "Janey wants to put her offspring to bed, Pete. We'd better go."

"If I can ever do anything for you on the same scale—" Jane said inadequately as she saw them out the front door, "though what it would be I just can't imagine—"

"Relax, Janey! It was a trifle. You get those kids to bed. Wouldn't do *you* any harm, either, to get an early night by the look of you."

Tom looked as if he had a mind to say something more, but then evidently thought better of it and strode rapidly up the dusky drive after his friend.

Graham did not get back until very late; Jane herself had not—in spite of Tom's admonition—managed to go to bed before eleven thirty, by the time the washing and the cooking for next day were finished. As soon as her head hit the pillow, she fell into deep, exhausted sleep, but even through it she was aware that a gap of two or three hours at least then elapsed before she heard the slam of the front door and was aware, through closed eyelids, of the reflection of light on her ceiling.

She had meant to ask Graham about the money next morning, but there was no time. He got up late, looking haggard and red-eyed, gulped down a cup of coffee, and left hurriedly while she was upstairs stripping the wet sheets from Caroline's bed.

Hearing the front door slam, Jane put her head out of the bedroom window and saw him lean for a moment over Donald's cot on the porch.

"Graham!" she called.

But he did not answer; perhaps he did not hear. He strode off to the garage.

"Daddy went without saying good-bye to us," Caroline commented, beside her mother at the window. "Why did he do that?"

"I suppose he was in a hurry to get to his office. Maybe he remembered some job that wanted doing fast."

"I wet my bed every night now, don't I?" Caroline remarked in the tone of one who hopes—though on slender grounds—to be contradicted.

"Never mind, lambie. You'll stop again by and by; then it will be more comfortable for you. How about taking Bear to bed with you?" Jane suggested, swiftly flinging clean sheets and blankets into position.

"Oh, no. Bear would hate to get wet."

"I don't believe he'd mind a bit. Damn, there comes Mrs. McGregor. That must mean it's a quarter past."

"Don't you like Mrs. McGregor?"

Truth or reassurance? Lie or troubling facts?

"I'd rather be at home looking after you myself, precious," Jane said, hugging her.

"Why aren't you?" The simple logic of childhood.

"Because we need the money I'm earning. Never mind. It won't be long now. Soon the job'll be over, and I'll be at home again."

"I wish it was now," Caroline said, her lip beginning to quiver as Mrs. McGregor and Susan approached.

AS USUAL, GRAHAM HAD LEFT A PILE OF BILLS UNOPENED; Jane took them to digest in the train. She was due a small dividend from her father's modest legacy next week, and she had formed the habit of settling such bills as she could, without attempting to break down the innumerable barriers of delay, argument, loss of bill, query of amount, and inquests over what constituted necessary and unnecessary expense, which were Graham's inevitable reactions to any demand that he should settle an account.

One of today's batch of cheap manila envelopes did not contain a bill. Opening it in the train, Jane found herself staring at a grubby slip of paper torn from a telephone memo pad, on which were the words: "Your WIFE is Carying on With Mstr Rolend" No signature, naturally.

Jane flipped the envelope over and studied it. Typed address. Two postmarks. 3p stamp stuck over a 2½p one. The envelope had evidently been taken out of a waste-paper basket and reused.

She read the short message again. It was meant for Graham, of course. What would he have thought if it had reached him?

Would he have been angry? Believed it? Or not cared?

Jane suddenly became aware of the eyes of the women sitting beside her, curiously studying the unpleasant little slip. Flushing, she folded and slid it into her handbag, with hands that shook a little.

Then it occurred to her that this might not have been the first such letter that had come. She felt sick and stared fixedly at the blurred landscape rushing past the train window. The worst feature of the whole business was the fact that the note had been written in Caroline's unmistakable toppling script.

What have I done, Jane thought, what could I ever have done, to make the woman detest me like that?

NEXT SUNDAY, FOR A WONDER, TURNED OUT FINE. THE WEEK- ends, so far as Jane was concerned, were an idyllic two days of respite from the McGregors. She played with the children, read to Caroline, wore her oldest jeans, and felt that the house belonged to her again.

But on this Sunday she was dismayed to see shortly after breakfast that McGregor, who now took a positively proprietorial interest in the garden, was out mowing the front lawn and that Mrs. McGregor and Susan, well wrapped up as usual, were sitting near him on a rug, Mrs. McGregor grimly knitting, Susan doing nothing.

Jane, who had been going out to sit in the sun herself, stopped short.

"Oh *lord!*" she said. "Do they have to come on Sunday, too? You'd think they had enough of this place in the week—that they'd be glad to stay at home weekends."

"Why on earth shouldn't they come?" Graham said irritably. "I expect McGregor thought he'd better get the grass cut while it isn't raining. It's very decent of him to give up his spare time. For heaven's sake, why must you carp at everything they do?"

His voice had the edginess of extreme strain; with compunction Jane noticed the dark shadows under his eyes. He was getting very thin too; and surely the gray hairs in his dark forelock were a new phenomenon?

"You're working too hard, Graham," she said. "Can't you ease off a bit?"

"Oh, don't nag me, Jane. I've got to keep going. You ought to know that."

She sighed; her eyes went back to Mrs. McGregor and Susan, sitting proprietorially on their rug, as if the garden were a public park. Like two fat slugs on a lettuce leaf. Parasites.

"I *wish* they hadn't come," she murmured, half to herself. "It does so spoil the day."

"You're being very ungenerous," Graham snapped. "It's extremely obliging of McGregor to work on a Sunday. And there's plenty of room in the garden for you as well. Do you grudge them a sit in the sun?"

"No, of course not. But I presume they've a garden of their own. And if I go out, I can hardly ignore them. I'll have to talk to them, make conversation."

"So? What's wrong with that? You're too grand to talk to the gardener's wife?"

Finding herself in an indefensible position, Jane gave up. Plum jumped on to her lap, purring his

60

raucous purr, and she hugged him absently, nerving herself for a frontal assault.

"Graham," she said. "Why haven't you paid Tom Roland for the mower yet?"

"I did—" he began.

But she went on swiftly, "I haven't been prying, honestly—I found out quite by chance the night before last, because Roland gave me a lift home, and he was saying he'd reduce the price because McGregor told him it wasn't working properly. Or, Tom said, he'd take it back if you prefer. Anyway I gathered that no money had changed hands."

"McGregor didn't say anything about its not working properly to *me*—I'd better go and ask him about it." With an air of urgency Graham stood up and started for the door.

But before he could escape, Jane said, "Never mind about that, for a moment, Graham. What's puzzling me is why you haven't paid Roland yet. What did you do with the money from Folia that I gave you?"

"I've still got it," Graham said evasively. "I was just going to pay him. Today, in fact. Anyway, I'll definitely settle with him next week if I don't see him today. In any case," he blustered, with a sudden show of indignation, "what the hell does it matter when I pay him? What business is it of yours?"

"I think it's some business of mine, since I provided the money."

"Isn't that just like a woman's logic! A real feminine bit of argument. I suppose you're worried that *your* friendly relations with Roland may be affected?"

"And what exactly do you mean by that?" Jane said quietly.

"What am I supposed to make of this, may I ask?"

With the air of a general bringing up a strategic

61

counterattack, he produced a slip of paper from his pocket.

Jane saw that it was identical with the one she had opened in the train.

"You know who's responsible for that, don't you?" she said. "Mrs. McGregor."

"Never mind who sent it," Graham said. "Is there any truth in it? That's what I'm asking."

His eyes, hostile, unhappy, angry, went from the ugly little message to Jane's face and back again.

"Of course it isn't true," she said flatly and coldly. "As you're well aware."

"I'm nothing of the sort"—his voice began to rise— "You do realize that any sort of unpleasant gossip around here might well do for me professionally? How am I supposed to tell what goes on around here in the evenings when I'm held up at Hastings? I gather that Roland and that Anstey who's always about with him were at this house the other evening. How many cozy sessions of that kind have there been?"

"You know perfectly well there haven't been any."

The sound of the mower had stopped some time since. Jane's eye caught a shadow on the window ledge. Gently depositing Plum on her chair, she moved to the window, glanced out, and saw McGregor diligently planting wallflowers in the narrow bed that ran along the side of the house. He straightened his back, gave her a brief glance, and strolled off at a slow, unconcerned pace.

She turned back to Graham. His face was flushed; he did not meet her eyes. She had the impression that all this worked-up indignation was really a cover to hide something else. Satisfaction? Relief? Or did he *want* her to be having a flirtation with Tom Roland?

"Oh, I can't stand this," Jane said suddenly and walked out of the room.

Plum sprang down and followed her, wailing.

In the front hall she met a dejected Caroline coming in from the garden, trailing Bear by one arm, and with her bit of pink blanket clutched against her cheek.

"Oh, stay outside, darling, won't you? It's so lovely and sunny for once."

"Don't want to," said Caroline. "Susan and her mummy's come. Anything I play with, Susan comes and takes it away."

Jane had, through the window, observed this trick of Susan's. Quietly, without particular malice or indeed any positive evidence of motive at all, but doggedly and continuously, she would follow Caroline from place to place, taking toys from her and then simply holding them in a silent, tenacious clutch.

"Oh, heavens," said Jane. "All right. I'll tell you what. We'll go for a bus ride. Quick! If we run like wild mustangs, we've just got time to catch the ten thirty."

She had discovered one wet afternoon six months before that the bus which ran past their gate to the railway station then continued in a long, meandering, figure-of-eight course, up through the little market town, along a hilly wooded ridge to a village about ten miles away called Fernden, and then back by a different route. It took over two hours and made a pleasant ride through hilly unspoilt country with a view of the sea at one point, thirty miles away across the rolling weald.

With any luck the McGregors would be gone by the time they got back.

As it was Sunday and there were no commuters, no shoppers, no school children, they had the bus to themselves except for an occasional short-distance passenger, in most cases elderly people off to spend Sunday with married children not far away. Jane sighed, thinking of her father, whom she still deeply missed. But he had liked Graham; he and Graham had got on very well.

"I hope you marry that chap. He's an able sort of character. He'll do well. He'll look after you," Professor Dillon had said as he died.

Even learned professors probably fall into a bit of wishful thinking when they die.

Caroline leaned happily against her mother, singing a tuneless song, hugging Bear, sucking her finger, gazing out of the window in dreamy content at the flowing green panorama of hopfield and oakwood, oakwood, oast houses, for drying the hops, and yet more hopfields.

"Like Plum," she remarked thoughtfully.

"What are, darling?" Jane said, coming out of her abstraction and thinking how like her grandfather Caroline often was.

"Those." Caroline pointed to another pair of oast houses. Jane could see what she meant. Their tipped cowls did have the alert, attentive air of the Siamese with his ears cocked, all his attention concentrated on a bird or grasshopper.

What could Graham possibly have done with all that money? Jane felt uneasily certain that he did not still have it. More and more of his activities nowadays seemed to be subterranean, completely concealed from Jane. Thinking back she tried to remember how long it was since he had freely told her things, been open with her. Had he ever really done so? When they first knew each other, his charm, his attentiveness, his total concentration on her (rather like Plum with the grasshopper), had been an impregnable surface, covering up aspects of himself which he had not wished to reveal.

64

What would happen if he were brought to a showdown?

It was like walking on lava. Jane had an undefined dread, which she hardly acknowledged to herself, that if she forced Graham to some disclosure—if the crust broke—the things she learned then would make a rupture almost inevitable. And then what? Her mind ran drearily along its familiar track: the children parted; Caroline necessarily left in the care of yet another stranger while Jane found another job—or maybe Folia would find her some other niche? Alimony from Graham? A hopeless notion; if she, here, now, on the spot, could not manage to get a square financial deal from him, what judge at long range would ever succeed in wresting regular payments out of him? And Donald? What would become of Donald? What sort of life would Graham lead if she left him?

Let things go on as they were then? But how could a person of any integrity blind themselves to such an atmosphere of concealment and withheld motives? Something was badly wrong, Jane was certain of it. She was almost sure that Graham had seized on the anonymous accusation against her and Tom Roland without in the least believing it simply as a convenient bulwark against any countercharge.

"Wish we had Donald with us," Caroline said, sucking her finger.

"Why, darling? He was fast asleep; it seemed a shame to wake him."

"Those are nice woods. We could have got out and had a picnic. Just us—you and me and Donald."

"And Daddy too."

"Daddy doesn't like picnics," Caroline said. "Just us would be best."

"All right. We will when I stop work. Or another Sunday."

"Next one?"

"All right. If it's fine."

That was why it hadn't occurred to her to do this before, of course, Jane thought, thinking back; no previous Sunday had been fine since Easter, it seemed. They lived in a shell of rain, like creatures in a diving bell, gazing out at a wet, alien world.

When the bus finally worked its way back to Culveden and they reluctantly walked up the long drive to the house, they found the interlopers still there in the garden, McGregor working steadily, like a man making good progress through a five-year plan.

Mrs. McGregor and Susan sat on their rug in what seemed exactly the same position that they had occupied two hours ago when Jane and Caroline left.

Graham lay in a deck chair, sunbathing. He tanned easily and took considerable pride in turning brown, even during a bad summer when everybody else was still bleached and pallid. Previously, in other summers, Jane had found this rather an endearing vanity. Now she was not so sure. Occasionally he would open his eyes and call out a suggestion, rather than an order, to McGregor; but these, so far as Jane could see, were treated with indifference or simply ignored.

As Jane and Caroline approached Graham, McGregor passed him, wheeling a barrow full of turf, walking with his silent, springy, loping tread. Passing within three feet of his employer, he looked down at him—Graham's eyes remained closed—and then went on, guiding the barrow easily over the uneven ground.

Jane hurried indoors, pulling Caroline with her, wondering what there had been in McGregor's look to shake her so abysmally. It had not been a threatening look, more—what was the right word? Affectionate? Proprietorial? Pitying? Like Plum, watching a grass-

66

hopper with fond, unwinking attention before he ate it?

Jane, keeping Caroline by her, prepared a cold lunch. She called Graham, woke Donald and fed him.

The McGregors picnicked in the garden. It was like having squatters, or gypsies encamped—a hostile tribe within the boundaries. They seemed to menace merely by their presence.

During the afternoon, McGregor worked doggedly on. Mrs. McGregor and Susan sat on their rug. Jane did some gardening herself; at a spot removed as far as possible from the other family, she planted a little herb bed with cuttings and seedlings that Tom had given her. Caroline, happy, absorbed, and earthy, helped.

Presently Graham came strolling down and glanced in a preoccupied way at their efforts.

"You must offer the McGregors tea," he said abruptly. "You can't ignore them all day."

Jane turned unwontedly stubborn. "I'm blowed if I will. I didn't invite them. They came of their own accord."

"Now get this straight, Jane—" Graham went white with anger. His hands shook slightly. "Once and for all, will you remember that I told you to be civil to the McGregors? It was bloody rude to go off like that this morning without saying a word to them. This afternoon I expect you to put that right. Will you kindly behave with a little common decency and give them tea?"

"No, I will not. There's only enough bread for breakfast. I'd have to make scones, and I'm not going to waste my Sunday afternoon doing that. Why in the world should I?"

"There's no need for such a palaver," he said impatiently. "Surely you can just give them a cup of tea and a biscuit?"

"I could if they hadn't already eaten all the biscuits. That's what they seem to live on, so far as I can see."

"Well, for God's sake you can find *something*. If you don't, they'll think you are a conceited, snobbish—"

"Have those McGregors got some sort of *hold* over you?" burst out Jane, impulsiveness overriding her usual prudence. "It's incredible, this need you feel to placate them. It can't just be an atavistic hark-back to the feudal pleasures of hiring labor." Another thought shot out before she could check it. "I suppose you didn't pay that money of mine to *McGregor*, by any chance?"

Graham's face stopped her short.

She turned around and saw Mrs. McGregor a few yards off, picking a way distastefully, in her stubby ladylike little shoes, through the ragged grass.

"It's coming on to drizzle a bit, madam," she said, ignoring Graham, fixing Jane with her pale eyes. "If you have no objection, Susan and I will sit in the kitchen till McGregor's finished his work, till he's ready to go home."

She was right, Jane noticed absently. A few drops were beginning to fall; it had been too much to hope that the fine weather might last.

"Do by all means," Jane said coldly. "Make yourselves some tea, why don't you? I'm sorry there's no cake or biscuits. I'm just going down to the village."

She turned, giving Graham a full clear look. Trapped, helpless, hating, his eyes met hers, then slid away.

For the second time that day Jane ran out on a situation. She took the children around to see Miss Ames (shoveling out of sight down at the bottom of her mind the faint hope that Tom Roland might also be there).

Miss Ames ran the China Bowl Café halfway down

68

the hill, combining this occupation in the summer months with a guest house for tourists. Here Jane and Graham had stayed for spells before and during the building of their house, and they had eaten a good many odd meals at the café since, while their own kitchen was still in its embryonic stages.

Miss Ames was a large pink-complexioned lady with tousled curly hair halfway between hay color and white. She always wore pale-blue nylon overalls over good tweeds, had strong vegetarian views, and found time among her other activities to spin, weave, play the recorder, and make artificial flowers out of twigs and foil bottle tops. She was kind, slightly mad, a first-rate cook, and ran her café with great efficiency. Theoretically it was closed on Sundays, but she never minded making an exception for a friend. Since she was very fond of Jane and the children, she welcomed them as if she had been hoping all day that they might turn up.

"We've come to hear how you enjoyed your holiday," Jane said.

"Oh, my dear child, I've never been so bored. Terrible weather. Glad to get back. And how's Caroline? Looking a little peaky—it's all this rain. Can you wonder? Are you coming in to the kitchen, Caroline, to help me carry the cakes? We'll see if we can find any raspberries, shall we?"

"Yes, please," said Caroline, and went with her confidently, while Jane, acting under orders, laid out handmade raffia mats and pottery plates.

"Dandelion tea or nettle?" Miss Ames called from the kitchen.

"Whichever is easier."

"Nettle then. It's an excellent crop this year."

Nettle tea was fiercely dark green and pungent. If

69

I drank this stuff all the time, Jane thought, sipping it cautiously, I might be tougher about taking some sort of action, coming to some sort of decision. . . .

Caroline climbed on to her mother's lap and leaned against her, sucking a finger.

"She sickening for something?" Miss Ames murmured in an undertone, her kind, shrewd, mad eyes taking in more at a glance than most people's did in a day.

Jane shook her head. "Just a little under the weather," she said softly.

"Aren't we all? You'll be glad when you finish that job of yours up in London. Ghastly place."

They were washing up the tea things when Tom Roland and Peter Anstey came in to buy cigarettes, and lingered for more extempore scenes from Goldilocks. Jane was surprised to find that she could take part, and abandon herself to the fooling, acting a lachrymose and fussy Mother Bear, capping Peter's terrible puns with even worse ones, dissociated and yet aware of the avalanche that awaited her at home.

"Why, child, you ought to be on the stage," Miss Ames said. "I'm surprised no one's ever made you into a film star."

"She hasn't the looks," Tom said seriously.

"Ah, come, she's not so bad. It's a taking little face."

"Shucks. I had plenty of offers—Rome, Hollywood, the lot," Jane boasted. "I just wouldn't leave the children."

"Leave me?" Caroline clung to her anxiously, instantly.

"We were joking, precious."

"Get along with the lot of you now," Miss Ames said. "I've all tomorrow's cakes to make."

Strolling up the hill towards home, a few yards behind Peter, who was pushing the pram and telling Caroline the tale of the big bad wolf, Tom said, "Janey, I should like to talk to you forever."

Jane swallowed. Silence enclosed her like a vacuum.

Finally she found voice enough to say, "What would happen to your television audiences in the meantime?"

"She has a tongue like a needle," Tom said to Peter, waiting with the children at the gate.

But his eyes met hers gravely.

A SMALL SILENT GROUP PUSHED PAST THEM THROUGH THE drizzle: the McGregors, homeward bound. McGregor gave Jane a formal nod; his wife, with Susan on the carrier of her bicycle, passed with eyes straight ahead, lips compressed. But missing nothing, Jane was sure. She said a brief good night to Peter and Tom, and hurried on down the drive.

Graham was withdrawn and lowering over supper, after she had put the children to bed. He ate little; Jane and he hardly exchanged more than three sentences in the course of the meal. Jane wondered whether to mention the broken teapot. It was her largest—a wedding-present Spode one, which she rarely used. It had been left out, in an ostentatious manner, with its spout beside it, on the kitchen counter. Bald honesty? Or deliberate malice? There was little doubt in Jane's mind. But she finally decided not to mention it. The pot was too heavy anyway, and dribbled as it poured; she had never liked it much. In any case it would be easy enough to mend with epoxy resin.

"Where's Plum?" she asked as she cleared away

the dishes. "He hasn't come in for his fish. Have you seen him anywhere?"

"No idea," Graham answered indifferently. He was not fond of cats. "Won't be far, I daresay. He was in the garden this afternoon."

Jane went to the back door and called, "Plum! Puss, puss, puss!"

"He'll come in his own good time," Graham said.

"I don't like him staying out at night when it's so wet. He catches cold terribly easily. And I just haven't time to inhale him with turpentine at the moment, if he should get one of his attacks."

"If you paid the attention to humans that you do to that cat—"

"I happen to love him and feel responsible for him," Jane said. "And he behaves as if he were fond of me."

She walked out into the wet dark, still calling. But Plum did not come in for his meal.

Refusing to let herself worry too much—after all, he was probably sheltering in the summerhouse, where he had been known to sleep all day, curled up on a heap of garden raffiia—Jane went to bed. The paperback anthology of verse she kept under her pillow for late-night reading had fallen down behind the head of the bed. Fishing for it, her fingers encountered a slip of pasteboard, as well as the book.

"This must be yours?" she said, puzzled, passing the photograph to Graham. "I can't think how it got down there."

He gave it a brief glance and then said with unnecessary emphasis, "It certainly is not mine. Never saw it before. It must have fallen out of your book."

"No. I only bought this book the other day, and it's been under my pillow ever since. Anyway, what would I be doing with a picture of a block of flats? And surely

72

one of the people in that group standing by the entrance is you?"

"No, it's not. How could you possibly tell at that distance, with the back turned, anyway?"

Jane sighed. "In that case, heaven knows how it came here. Maybe Mrs. McGregor dropped it. Though I can't imagine what she'd have been doing in here today."

"It could have been under the bed for days."

"No, it couldn't. I vacuumed this room today. Oh, well, it doesn't matter. I'll try and remember to ask her tomorrow."

Jane rolled over and switched off her light. Graham made a sound of protest, then checked himself.

"I've got a headache," he said. "Going to walk it off. Then I think I'll sleep in the study."

Jane was asleep by the time he went to bed.

SHE FORGOT ABOUT THE PHOTOGRAPH NEXT MORNING. FOR conducting a hasty search in the garden for the cat after breakfast, she found him stretched out under a clump of brambles. He was caught in one of the rabbit snares that McGregor had put down, without asking permission, at the wilder end of the land. Plum had been dead for some time, but it had been a slow and painful death; he had struggled a great deal.

Hearing Caroline coming, Jane hastily hid the cat's body deeper in the bramble thicket, swallowed hard against tears and nausea, and tried to think how and when to break the news to the child. Not now. It would be best, perhaps, to say Plum had been taken ill in the night, that Graham had taken him off to the vet's surgery, that he was receiving every care. Then, later, the fact of his death could be filtered through. . . . She hated lying to Caroline but here, surely, a lie was better than the gruesome truth just before the day's parting?

She would bury the body that evening after Caroline was in bed.

Later, at the office, she began to wonder if Plum's death had been an accident or not? The teapot, she was fairly sure, had been a deliberate act. But would somebody in cold blood kill a gentle, beautiful, and inoffensive animal?

McGregor could, she thought.

". . . Jane?" said the thin girlish voice on the office line. "Oh, good, I'm so glad I found you. Graham told me the other night that you were back at Folia for a spell. How are you? Having fun?"

Without waiting for an answer, the voice went on. "Listen—can I ask a favor? You're the only possible person I can turn to. I'm in the most awful fix. Can you possibly come to the rescue?"

"Of course, Ellie."

Despite her low spirits, Jane could not suppress a slight interior grin. For when was Ellie not in a fix? Pretty, feather-pated, blonde as a dandelion clock, she drew trouble as a white carpet attracts mud. Dozens of times in the last five years Ellie had rung up in a state of desperation, asking for succor and advice. Mostly it was disastrous love affairs with married men;

then she had made a series of appalling gaffes while interviewing for an independent television program; once it had been an accusation of embezzlement, due to the hopeless muddle in which she had kept some charitable organization's accounts; once she was being sued for libel after she had contributed an incautious article to an underground magazine; once she had wanted to hide from the Queen's Proctor; once it was Breach of Promise ("I *never* promised him," Ellie had declared, half tearful but half laughing. "I never, never, promise *anything*"); once she had arrived in terror in a taxi, declaring that a sinister bearded man had followed her all the way from Cambridge to the southern suburbs of London.

Jane took all these stories with a large dose of salt, since Ellie contrived, by some means or other, to glide out of every predicament without assault, damages, injunctions, or huge black headlines in the Sunday tabloids. But still it seemed probable that one day disaster would really catch up with her; whether deserved or undeserved, it would no doubt be hard to decide. She was sweet-natured, silly, and harmless as a rice bun. Even Graham grudgingly admitted that of all Jane's acquaintances she was the least highbrow or intellectually snobbish, and the easiest to get on with. He was even, Jane thought, quite fond of her. Ellie on her side was a little in awe of Graham's moodiness and his sulky Restoration good looks; she referred to him gigglingly as "the Man of Wrath" and tended to be very humble and placating with him, all sweet deference, suppressing any opinions she herself might possibly hold.

"After all, we've got to *live* with men," she had once said to Jane. "No point in treading on their toes all the time, even if they *do* have as many toes as a centipede. It's just not sensible to quarrel with a man, darling. There's only one thing to do if it's got to *that* stage, which is to leave him, as fast as possible.''

Whom would she be leaving now? It was some time since Everard—he had been a Tory M.P. with an indignant wife. Then there had been Amos, a kindhearted romantic West Indian doctor, who had rushed back to Trinidad with a broken heart; then there had been the Yoga interlude with some vegetarian community on the Norfolk coast—Ellie had been expelled from there for beguiling the guru from his contemplation. Then who? Jane had rather lost track. It was in fact quite a time since they had seen Ellie.

''What's the trouble, duck?''

''You needn't bother to add *this time*. I can hear it in your voice,'' Ellie said, laughing. ''Sweetie, I can't possibly tell you over the phone, but the thing is, could I possibly come and stay with you next weekend? My landlady's throwing me out—in fact, she's thrown me—and I've simply got to pour out my troubles to someone and think what to do next, and you're such a tower of sense.''

''Of course, you can. Delighted to have you. Come tonight if your landlady's thrown you out.''

''Oh, you are a love. I won't come tonight, because I've got to collect some things of mine from a place in Golder's Green''—Ellie's possessions were always mysteriously scattered about London, on loan to even more improvident friends, or left behind after some extra-quick flit, or sent ahead to some hoped-for refuge which then slammed its doors in her face— ''but I'll be all right for two or three nights; I'm fairly sure Wendy and Alec will put me up. I'll see you on Friday then. I'll travel down with you, shall I? What train do you usually catch?''

Jane told her. "Lovely to see you, Ellie," she said and hung up, anxious to get on with the pile of work waiting for her. In fact, she thought, Ellie's presence would act as a useful emollient to the strained relations existing between herself and Graham. Three can be easier than two. Probably Ellie will cheer him up, Jane thought.

She was wrong. Unexpectedly, he was not at all pleased when Jane told him that Ellie was coming. In fact, he flew into a rage.

"*That* blasted nitwit of a girl? What does she want to come down here for? Really," he went on, working himself up to an even higher pitch of indignation, "it's almighty cool the way she just invites herself, without any regard for our convenience at all. You're working quite as hard as you should. Why did you let her?"

"I like Ellie. It'll be nice to see her."

"Well, it's just bloody not convenient now—with the McGregors, and your job, and—and everything. Tell her she can't come. We can't have her after all."

"No, why should I? I'm looking forward to seeing her."

"Then *I'll* tell her," said Graham angrily.

"You'll do no such thing!" Jane exclaimed. And she added clinchingly, "Anyway, it's out of the question. I don't know her address. She's just left her old digs."

Graham opened his mouth to speak, shut it again, and walked out of the room without further remark.

Then Jane remembered that she had meant to ask what had happened to the mysterious photograph. In the course of the day it had vanished from where she had left it, perched on the bedroom mantelpiece. Perhaps it had been Mrs. McGregor's after all, though a picture of a block of flats seemed an unlikely possession for her. And why should she have dropped it under the bed? The thought that she had been in that room at all was curiously unpleasant.

Really it was more likely that the print had been Graham's. Perhaps he had just been lying about it. Jane felt sure that he was lying to her half the time nowadays. I ought to ask him about it, she thought vaguely. There are too many things that I am not tackling as I ought.

But she was so tired. Most of the time now she felt literally dragged towards the ground with tiredness, as if the law of gravity operated more heavily on her than on anyone else. Each bone, each muscle, seemed to suffer the downward pull separately; the impulse just to crawl up to bed after supper had to be fought every day afresh—as now. After the unhappy task of burying Plum she washed the dishes, cooked a joint of bacon, made potato salad, fruit salad, left vegetables ready for cooking; at least she could see that the children had an adequate diet, not just tinned stuff and biscuits.

I suppose, she thought with a weary flash of self-criticism, all this cooking is in protest against Mrs. McGregor's ostentatious housework.

By now the house had reached a fanatical, aggressive peak of cleanliness which it would never achieve again in Jane's lifetime. Polish had been applied like war paint. Furniture was arranged with obsessional neatness; tired as she was, it took a conscious effort of will on Jane's part not to wander round in the evening moving everything to its normal, comfortable, casual state. But there was the washing still to be tackled. . . .

Caroline seemed to have got through an ominous number of pairs of pants in the course of the day. Did she wet herself in the daytime now, as well as at night? Dragging out the washing machine, absorbed in this new worry, Jane forgot the photograph of the block of flats.

"I'LL HAVE TO ASK FOR AN INCREASE IN MY PAY, MADAM," Mrs. McGregor said on Thursday, her lips primmed together as she disparagingly inspected the food that had been left for lunch.

"Oh? Why is that?" Jane glanced at her watch. Four minutes to catch the bus.

"It's Caroline, madam." The *miss* had been dropped, Jane noticed.

"What's the matter?" Jane asked with sinking heart.

"She's both wet and dirty as often as not, now, madam. I should not be expected to clear up after her without getting paid extra for it."

And if she is, it's entirely due to your mismanagement of her, you hateful harpy. Before your advent, Caroline was a happy, serene, intelligent child, slightly ahead of her age-group. Now—after six weeks—

But there were now only two minutes to bus time.

"You'll have to speak to my husband about it. He's the one who makes the decisions," Jane said. She tightly hugged the speechless, tearful Caroline, and ran down the drive.

A resolve was forming in her mind. She could not stop working for Folia before the end of the agreed period; for one thing she could not let them down, and in any case she had already been paid, and there was no possible chance of getting the money back from Graham—she was certain of that. But she could find an alternative to Mrs. McGregor.

That evening, when she came home, she walked up the garden to the sound of singing. Three voices were hauntingly twined together in a strange air with a lilting, insistent beat. Jane stood outside a moment, caught off-guard by sheer pleasure; then she went on and opened the door.

The singing broke off at once. The McGregors began in silence to gather up their belongings. Their hostility towards Jane was now quite unconcealed.

"Oh, I wish you hadn't stopped!" Jane was glad to be able to say something sincerely friendly for once. "It was so beautiful. What was it?"

Nobody answered. Mrs. McGregor was buttoning Susan's knitted woolen leggings. Although it was now muggy July weather, the child's clothes were still more suited to midwinter. McGregor stood half whistling, with his back to them, looking out of the window.

Jane had the impression that they would have preferred her not to hear, not to enjoy their singing; as plainly as words their silence indicated profound contempt for her ignorant, facile enthusiasm. And yet they must have known that she was bound to hear the music as she came in.

"I was sorry to hear about the cat, madam," McGregor said. He spoke softly and civilly, but there was not a shred of real sympathy in his tone. When the narrow black eyes met hers, Jane knew that she had been right in her guess about Plum.

"It was a good thing, though, really, wasn't it," Mrs. McGregor said smoothly. "Vicious, he was, that cat. Two or three times he'd scratched my Susan; next thing, for all we know, he'd very likely have got in the pram and savaged Master Donald."

Jane kept silent with an effort.

"Oh, I'm afraid Caroline's in disgrace again,

madam, for the number of pairs of panties she's wetted during the day. I told her we shall have to cut down on her drinks. She's upstairs in her bedroom.''

Mrs. McGreggor stepped out and gently closed the front door behind her.

Thank God, thank God, Jane thought; only one more week to go.

ELLIE, CONTRARY TO EXPECTATION, WAS AT CANNON STREET on time, caught the train, and traveled down with Jane on Friday evening. As usual on a Friday the train was packed with extra weekend commuters; Ellie and Jane had to stand in the corridor, jammed like sardines between the other travelers, and it was not possible to be confidential. Ellie, Jane thought, looked desperately white and tired. There were shadows under her huge guileless gray eyes, and she was thinner than ever; her wrists were like chicken bones.

In the station yard at Culveden, Jane saw Tom Roland battling his way through the Friday night mob. As always, her heart rose at sight of him—he was so cheerful, dynamic, sensible, reliable. If things get any worse, she thought, carefully not framing to herself exactly what she meant by *things,* I'll ask Tom's advice about it all. That's it; I'll ask Tom.

''Lift, Janey?''

The warmth of his smile was like a fire on a freezing day.

''There are two of us today. I've got a friend with me. Have you room?''

''Of course.''

Jane looked round for Ellie and saw her a few yards away, staring at Tom. Her face was gray, drawn, a mask of appalled recognition. She stood limply, like someone about to hear sentence of death.

"Ellie, this is Tom Roland our neighbor, who's offered us a lift home. Tom, my friend Ellie Rostrevor, who works for *Epitome*."

"Not any more," Ellie found voice enough to say. "They sacked me. Didn't I tell you?"

"Oh, too bad. Still, it didn't look like a magazine with much of a future to me. I'm sure you could do better—"

Jane was surprised to see that the smile had died out of Tom Roland's eyes. He looked blank, as if uncertain how to proceed. But he shook hands politely, and put Ellie's hold-all in the trunk, and started the car, while Jane kept up a random conversation in order to drown the uneasy silence.

"Ellie and I are each other's oldest friends, Tom. We were at school together. She was the untidiest girl in the school. We used to say that she'd simply have to marry a duke—"

It was an uncomfortable ride. Tom dropped them at the gate and drove off with a brief wave of his hand for Jane. She felt deprived. It was the first time she had seen him since Sunday. She had been prepared for some constraint, but not of this kind. For a moment she felt unwonted impatience with Ellie. What had the silly girl done, asked him the wrong question on some panel program? It was obvious, though neither said so, that they must have met before.

Mrs. McGregor was alone in the kitchen with Susan when they got in.

"Where's Caroline?" Jane asked at once.

"She burned herself, madam," Mrs. McGregor said. "I put her to bed."

82

"*Burned* herself—how?"

"On the iron, madam. Pulled it down on herself. I've told her ever so many times not to go near it. I told her she was a naughty girl—"

"Did you get the doctor?"

"Oh, no, madam. It's not a bad burn."

Jane flew upstairs. Caroline was in bed, restless and flushed from crying. The burn, a fairly severe one, though certainly not so much so as to justify sending for the doctor, was on her forearm.

"How did it happen, honey?" Jane said as she put on a dry dressing.

"I don't know."

"But, lambie, you *must* know—a bad burn like that? Did you trip over the iron cord? Did the iron fall on you? You weren't trying to iron something yourself?"

Jane glanced at the warm towel rail. A row of Caroline's little pairs of cotton pants from yesterday hung on it. Mrs. McGregor, fanatical in this as in all else, insisted on ironing underwear though Jane had told her for heaven's sake not to bother.

"Did the iron fall on you?" Jane repeated.

"I don't know," insisted Caroline. "Don't know, don't know, I tell you." She burst into a storm of tears and flung herself against Jane.

"Never mind, never mind, my precious. Don't worry about it. It doesn't matter." Jane was appalled at the note of desperation in her crying. "Here—where's Pinkie? Let's find him for you to cuddle, and then you'll feel better."

Caroline's tears turned to hysterical wails. "Pinkie —all gone—" Her words were so stifled and choked with sobs that it took a while for Jane to understand. "All gone—all burned up. Mrs. McGregor burned Pinkie—"

"Mrs. McGregor did *what*?"

"In the stove—burned him—to teach me not to be a naughty girl—"

Black rage boiled over in Jane. Was *that* how Caroline had been burned? In some struggle? She turned to rush down the stairs, but then checked herself. First things first.

"Never mind, my precious. That was a horrid, stupid thing to do, but I know where there's another Pinkie. Hang on just a tick—"

From the bottom drawer of her wardrobe she hastily rummaged out the reserve half of Caroline's pink fetish-blanket and worked it into the arms of her sobbing child.

"*Look*—every bit as good as the other one. Only just a little cleaner. Now, I'm going to say a word to Mrs. McGreg—"

But at that moment she heard the front door slam and Ellie's voice calling good night. In any case, comforting Caroline was more important. She applied herself to that.

After five minutes Caroline was calmed down enough to take interest in an offer of glucose.

"Mummy," she said when Jane came back with the cup. "I want to whisper something."

"What, lambie?"

Caroline glanced fearfully around the room and then whispered, "Please don't let Mrs. McGregor and Susan come any more. Please don't!"

"It's only for one more week, darling. Only five days."

But from Caroline's expression she could see that to the child five days were the equivalent of a life sentence.

"Well—I'll see what I can do. I'll see. I promise."

The look on Caroline's face remained with her as she ran downstairs.

"Sorry to abandon you so abruptly, Ellie."

"Oh, lawks, love, don't you worry about me. Is Caroline going to be okay? What a rotten thing to happen, poor angel. Shall I go and talk to her?"

"Yes, do Ellie. That would be sweet of you. She loves you. Have a beer to take up with you? I'm afraid we don't run to sherry at present."

"What, in spite of your job and all Graham's connections, you plutocrats?" But there was little heart in Ellie's teasing. "No, truly, beer will suit me fine. *I've* been living on *bread and water* since the end of last month."

Ellie was always in dire straits of poverty—when she was not spending a month on somebody else's expense account at the Istanbul Hilton. But this time she really did look undernourished and run down. Jane glanced after her in vague surprise as she walked slowly up the stairs with the glass of beer in her hand. Ellie usually ran everywhere; at some point in her varied career she had put in a spell of ballet training and was light-footed as a grasshopper.

Graham would not be coming home tonight; he was staying in Hastings, as he had done several times in the last few weeks. Jane had intended to take it easy with bread and cheese for the evening meal, but she changed her mind and, to get a bit of nourishment into Ellie, substituted soup, omelette, and a salad.

"Had you and Tom met before?" she asked as they washed up afterwards.

"No, never, that I know of," Ellie said carelessly—too carelessly.

"I thought you seemed to know him."

"I've seen him on television of course. Often. Does he live round here?"

"Just down the road," Jane answered slowly. She felt sure Ellie was lying. And she felt sure that Ellie had never lied to her before—some of her more hair-raising disclosures she had laughingly skirted around, saying there was no need to horrify Jane unduly, but she had always been completely frank if asked an outright question. So what new development was this?

Suppose I were to ask Tom if he met Ellie before? How would he answer?

But that idea threw such a disturbing light on her relationship with Tom—not relationship with, she told herself, attitude towards—that Jane preferred to shelve it. Besides, what right had she to go interrogating Tom about whom he knew or didn't know?

None. None.

And what sort of relationship—attitude—permitted suspicions that people had met before and, for some reason, were concealing the acquaintance?

Dealing with the McGregors—and—and Graham is making me pathologically suspicious, Jane decided.

GRAHAM WAS NOT EXPECTED HOME UNTIL THE EVENING OF the next day. Saturday turned out to be another rare, fine day in that brooding, thunderous summer. Jane and Ellie spent most of it in the garden with the children. Caroline was still subdued from the pain of her burn, content to play cat's cradle with Ellie and be read aloud to. Donald, a peaceful, unenterprising baby, lay kicking on a rug in the sun, thought about trying to roll over, decided against it. The McGregors stayed away. So did Tom. Nobody came near the house all day.

Jane, looking around her at the trees and grass, the distant watery gleam of the weir (Had McGregor re-

86

paired the gaps in the fence yet? He had not; damn
him) thought: Take them away from all this tranquillity
and beauty? How could I? Only another week to go, and
then, when I'm not so tired, I'll somehow get things
sorted out with Graham, establish a better relationship,
more confidence on each side. If I get him to tell me
what's worrying him, that's the main thing. That,
and getting rid of the McGregors.

Ellie was not communicative. She told stories to Caroline, but said little to Jane. She, too, seemed to be
resting and gathering strength. Whatever her problem,
she had not yet screwed herself up to the point of con-
fiding it.

Towards suppertime, Graham still had not appeared,
but Ellie said she was fairly sure she had seen him
walk past the house and down towards the bottom of
the garden.

Jane, irritated by this casual behavior—he might at
least have come in to say he was home—went out to
summon him. She was fairly sure that this avoidance
was a deliberate affront to herself, to demonstrate that
he didn't want Ellie as a visitor. Otherwise he would
have been sure to come in and see Donald's bath; it
was the one bit of Saturday routine he never missed.

"I shan't be a moment, Ellie. Just stay within ear-
shot of Caroline, could you? It's awful. She used to be
so angelic about going to bed. Never wanted anything
once she was settled—"

"She'll be perfectly okay again once you're at
home," Ellie said comfortingly.

The day's promise had dwindled by tea time into the
usual gray despondency which had presently turned
to drizzle and then to no-nonsense rain. Jane put on
rubber boots and swished through the long wet grass
down the slope that led to their rear boundary.

A row of willow trees partly concealed the water meadows that lay beyond. Under one of these trees Graham had built himself a primitive wooden studio-summerhouse, which he called his hermitage. In it, he declared, when he was affluent and successful, he would do all his work, and clients could visit him there. It commanded a beautiful view of fields, trees, water, and nothing else.

Jane thought he must be in it now; he was not to be seen anywhere else about the garden, and anyway it was now pouring rain. But hiding himself from her and Ellie—sulking? What a childish piece of behavior.

Pushing open the door, she put her head around. "Graham?"

Inside the cabin it was almost dark, but she had been right; she could see his head outlined against the window.

"Graham? What *are* you doing down here? Supper's been ready for ages. Ellie's here, don't forget. And listen—do please try and—"

He rose and took two steps towards her. His attitude was so menacing that she flinched back. Then, to her astonishment, his arms went around her; he held her in a rigid grip.

"What in heaven's—" began Jane confusedly; and then, "No! Stop it!"

Thin, cold lips—not Graham's—pressed violently down on hers. She could feel the teeth behind them, and the bone of his ribs, smell the smell of earth and old wet leather jacket, and skin and hair, sweaty, sharply, acidly metallic. It was like encountering a wild animal in its burrow.

She struggled frantically, from shock more than fright. But fright was there, too. At last, with insulting ease and slowness, he released her and held her off at arm's length, both wrists in one hand. His grip was of paralyzing strength; she gritted her teeth at the pain and indignity.

"I'm sorry, madam." The soft voice was at ironic odds with the inflexible, bruising grip. "I'm afraid I forgot myself. I expect you thought I was Mr. Drummond, eh? Or did *you* forget yourself, too?"

But that was the extraordinary thing. For a couple of seconds—no more—she *had* thought he was Graham.

She made some sound of protest.

"It was all a big mistake then. We won't mention this to Mr. Drummond, shall we?" he softly suggested.

In the fractional pause that followed, a whole possible future for Jane lay balanced, and was decided as she answered coldly, "I certainly shall tell Mr. Drummond about it. I don't keep secrets from him. Will you please shut the door as you leave. The rain is coming in."

She walked swiftly back towards the house. She could hear McGregor padding through the grass behind her, but she did not look around. She could not endure the thought of his face.

Just as she reached the back door, his voice came again. "Madam: Suppose I come up and we have a talk about this some time when Mr. Drummond's away?"

She opened the door without replying.

Softly and menacingly he said, "I really shouldn't tell him if I was you, madam. You may not have secrets from Mr. Drummond, but he has plenty from you. I don't think you'd be wise to upset him."

Without making any answer, she walked indoors.

She heard his bicycle clink on a stone as he rode off up the drive.

Graham had returned home, she discovered, while she had been down the garden. He and Ellie stood on either side of the kitchen stove in the arrested attitudes of two people interrupted in a furious argument. Neither spoke as Jane dished up the meal. Only, when she went to the larder for butter, she heard Graham mutter in a savage whisper, "Cheat!"

Ellie's reply, if she made one, was inaudible. As she sat down at table, her lip was quivering, her face flushed; she looked about fourteen.

It was a silent meal until about halfway through, Jane, out of patience with Graham's surly monosyllabic quenchers to her efforts at conversation, said suddenly, "Ellie, you don't look a bit well. Couldn't you stay down here for a couple of weeks, if you've left the magazine? Honestly you don't look fit to go back to town."

"Well—it would be *marvelous*—" Ellie began doubtfully, her eyes flying to Graham.

"Listen, Graham!" Jane turned to him. "I might as well tell you now, I simply can't stand the McGregors about the place a single day more. Caroline's scared to death of them. I don't know what Mrs. McGregor does to her, but I strongly suspect that burn on her arm was deliberate. I think the woman's a real sadist. If they come down tomorrow, you must tell them they aren't wanted any more. Or else I'll drop a note at their house. They'll have to have a week's wages in lieu of notice. The job's over. Ellie, you could cope with the children for a week, couldn't you, if I leave everything all ready for you, the way I've been doing for that awful woman? You haven't got a new job lined up?"

Ellie shook her head.

"Are you mad?" said Graham savagely. "Are you clean out of your mind? I tell you, we've got to keep the McGregors on. *Got* to, understand? It's not a question of your blasted silly likes and dislikes. It's my whole future. And we're going to need a whole lot more money—you'll have to ask Folia if you can stay on there. If not, you must start looking for a permanent job next week.

"As for *you*"—he turned his bloodshot eyes on Ellie —"I don't know why you were so pigheadedly stupid as to force your way down here. There's nothing for you here, nothing at all, so you might as well get that into your brainless skull. I'm certainly not having you looking after Donald, and that's flat. So just paddle back to your gutter, will you?"

With a histrionic gesture he stood up, pushing away his half-finished plate of food, and said. "I'm going around to the pub. I'll be back late. I expect Tom will be there."

"Tom drove us home from the station yesterday," Ellie said softly.

Graham stared at her for a moment, then fumbled for the door handle and went out, slamming the door behind him.

After a moment's silence Ellie collapsed forward over the table, her head on her arms. Great coughing sobs shook her thin body.

"*Don't*, Ellie," Jane said, deeply distressed. "Don't cry so. Whatever the trouble is, it's not so bad as that."

She came over to Ellie and put an arm around the shaking shoulders.

"Don't let Graham upset you. He's got something on his mind. He's been in a filthy temper for weeks, but it's nothing to do with you. He'd be like that to the Queen of Sheba if I had her for the weekend. He'll come out with whatever's bothering him in the end: the firm's probably bankrupt or something. But it's not *your* worry. Graham's just taking it out on me, that's his way. He's always telling me that you're the nicest of my friends—he's really fond of you."

Ellie's sobs continued; she made no answer. Jane went on soothing and patting.

A couple of moments later, she heard what seemed to be a step in the nursery overhead, and raised her head in disquiet. Graham had said he was going out. Had he changed his mind? Or was it Caroline? Once or twice lately Jane had found her wandering at night, sleepwalking—it was another worrying manifestation of the disturbed state she was in.

Leaving Ellie, Jane stole quietly upstairs and looked into the children's room.

What she saw troubled her more deeply than any somnambulistic activity of Caroline's could have done.

Graham, instead of storming off round to the pub, had apparently changed his mind and gone upstairs instead. He was kneeling hunched by Donald's cot, one arm thrown over the hump of blanket which was all that was visible of the sleeping baby. Jane could not see his face, but his whole despairing position wrung her heart.

Donald's the only being that he doesn't feel has betrayed him, she thought.

A rush of compunction, affection, urged her forward, prompted her to say something that might help bridge the gap between them. Then she hesitated. Let him have his moment with Donald. Later, she thought, I'll do it when he comes to bed. I won't break in on him now. She stole away as quietly as she had come.

Downstairs Ellie, having stacked the supper dishes, was watching television. Her unquenchable gaiety had bubbled up again like a spring; she was laughing wholeheartedly at a comedy program and seemed to have no connection with the sobbing, shattered girl of fifteen minutes before. Jane marveled at this vitality, as she had done on many occasions before, but packed her off to bed as soon as the program was over, pleading tiredness herself. In fact, worn down with bewilderment and worry, she found Ellie's high spirits hard to bear.

"Don't lie awake brooding," she advised. "Take a sleeping pill. Graham got some a couple of months ago. You'll find them in the bathroom cupboard—Dormason. They're pretty mild. Tomorrow we'll have a proper talk, shall we?"

Ellie did not reply directly. She said, "Good night, Janey darling. You're a saint."

Jane turned away, heavyhearted. She wished that Ellie had not picked up that particular nickname.

Finding a pile of mending, she sat herself doggedly down to work; she knew that she would not be able to sleep herself for a long time yet.

Half an hour later she crept up to look into Ellie's room and see if she was all right. The light was still on, but the sound of peaceful breathing came from the bed; evidently Ellie had gone right off to sleep. The bedside table held an empty glass and a half-empty flask of whiskey. Jane stared at it in dismay. Solitary drinking was not like Ellie, or so she would have said before today. How little one knew about people really—even the people one looked on as close friends.

She turned off the light and went back to her mending.

In the end she went to bed herself.

She was still lying awake when Graham came up, hours later. Jane thought he must have been out walking, or sitting in his studio. When he climbed into bed, she could feel an aura of chill come from him, as if he had been in the rain, and his hair was wet.

"Graham?" she said softly.

"Oh, God, are you awake?"

"Listen, Graham," she said. "I'm desperately serious about the McGregors. Caroline's really in a bad way; she can't take any more. Nor can I. It's not only Caroline—I feel they are doing awful, irremediable harm to both of us—to the whole family. There's something evil about the pair of them, I'm sure of it. And he—he kissed me tonight. Oh, I know it sounds stupid —trivial—but it wasn't. I'm terrified of him.''

"Kissed you?'' Graham said in a dead voice.

"In your studio. At first I thought it was *you*—that was the extraordinary thing. You must, you *must,* agree to get rid of him. After all it's not as though he had any claim on us—''

"Doesn't have any claim,'' Graham said. He sat up, switched the light on, and stared at Jane. "Hasn't any claim? You're terrified of him? What do you think I am? Do you know who that man is?''

"No, of course I don't,'' Jane said, trembling. "What do you mean? How could I? Who is he?''

"He's my brother—that's all.''

"Your *brother?* You said you were an orphan—an only child. Your mother—in Scotland—Are you joking?''

"Is it likely?'' He gave a short laugh. There was no amusement in the sound. "You see, my dear Jane, my background isn't quite what I represented to your dear old father when we met. When you step out of a slum, you want to leave it behind. It was just too bad that my slum managed to catch up with me again. Having a brother who's done time for armed robbery is hardly likely to recommend me to clients round here, is it?''

"Armed robbery?'' Jane said dazedly.

"Tim did a stretch for coshing a night watchman when he was nineteen.''

"Tim?'' Somehow the name so familiarly spoken

94

convinced her as nothing before had. "He really *is* your brother?"

"Half brother. He was brought up next door to us in Glasgow by a woman called Auntie Phemie. I always thought he was my cousin. In fact, as I discovered in my teens, Auntie Phemie was no aunt at all, just a friend; and Tim was my mother's son—my illegitimate younger half brother. My father didn't like Tim at all. Felt him as a personal affront, I daresay. When he was drunk—my father, I mean—he used to bawl at my mother on the subject of Tim's objectionable existence. Then after one of those spells Father went out and fell under a goods truck—he was a platelayer, worked on the railway. So after his death my mother had Tim to live with us. She was very fond of him—devoted, you might say. But Tim wasn't at all bright; he was a bit of a wild lad. I was the brains of the family."

"Good heavens." Jane murmured the words to herself; she lay silent, assimilating this revelation, which was on such a scale that it seemed to fill the whole dark room, the whole house.

"He thinks he's got me absolutely nailed down," Graham was saying.

"But why? It's not *your* fault he went to jail. And people aren't such snobs that they'd let something about a man's brother weigh with them—"

But even as she said it, she realized that there must be more in the background than that—much more. Where, for instance, did Tim's wife fit into the picture—Myfanwy? And the money?

You may not have secrets from Mr. Drummond, but he has plenty from you.

"Is your name not really Drummond, then?" she asked.

"Deed poll." Graham rolled over, savagely batter-

95

ing his pillow. "Otherwise *you*'d be Mrs. McGregor too, just like your pet aversion. Dear little Susan's your niece. Ironic, isn't it? All that madam and sir stuff is their idea of a joke. Tim knows things about me that I just can't afford—"

"What sort of things?" Jane asked as he came to a stop.

"Oh, about my first wife, for instance."

"First wife?"

"We all got married together. She was Myfanwy's sister."

"*Sister?*"

"Look, don't keep repeating everything I say, Jane, will you? She's dead anyway," he said shortly. Suddenly he reached up and switched off the light.

"So we aren't bigamously married. That's a comfort anyway," Jane said, trying for a lighter note and failing. "When you came to Malta—?"

"She'd died a year before."

"Where were Tim and his wife then?"

"He was in prison. I think she'd gone back to her family in Wales."

"In prison still? Or again?"

"Again. Will you *stop* cross-examining me?" he burst out. "I'm tired as hell. I'm not going to talk about it any more—now or ever probably. I just wanted you to know the basic thing, to stop you making any more of a fool of yourself. So now do you see why we have to keep on the right side of them?"

"But Graham, we haven't—"

No use. He rolled away from her, dragging the bedclothes up to his chin, so that Jane was half uncovered, and refused to say another word. She was sure he did not actually go to sleep for a long time, but at last his breathing lengthened and steadied.

96

Jane could not follow his example. She lay awake, hour after hour, staring at the graying sky, while slow, cold tears trickled backwards into the roots of her hair.

SHE FELL INTO A SHORT, HEAVY EXHAUSTED SLEEP NOT long before it was time to get up. The click of the door woke her. She found that Graham must have already risen, got dressed, and gone out. Where? To the studio? She had a whole series of questions she intended to ask, but now was not a suitable moment to pursue him. The baby had woken and was crying; Caroline was hungry, and her burn needed redressing.

Ellie slept right through the children's breakfast, and was pale and heavy-eyed when Jane later took her up a cup of coffee and glass of orange juice. Jane persuaded her to stay in bed till lunchtime, hoping that an affectionate smile and the Sunday papers would serve as sufficient evidence of sympathy and goodwill until she had gathered herself together a little more. She felt that listening with constructive attention to Ellie's problems would be more than she could manage just now.

She had woken in the vague hope that Graham's disclosures had all been some particularly awful dream, or a macabre bit of teasing on his part, but the barest thought had destroyed that hope. It all hung together: McGregor's hauntingly familiar appearance, the name Drummond—Hadn't that been a pseudonym for McGregor in proscription days? Graham's mother, Jane now remembered, had been called Susannah. Had there been any property left when she died? It seemed unlikely. Graham certainly had very little money when he married Jane. But if he had inherited anything from his mother, that would be one reason for Tim's hostile attitude. She felt quite certain that he begrudged Graham every single one of his possessions.

Caroline went up to Ellie's room when Jane carried her a lunch tray, and stayed there while Ellie lunched and then got up and dressed. Graham still had not appeared.

Leaving the pair of them peacefully occupied, Ellie brushing Caroline's hair and plaiting it in ribbons, Jane went down to see if Graham was in the studio. But it was empty; coming back, she found the car gone. Perhaps Graham was comforting himself by a survey of the building progress at Hastings. At least in his work he was capable; no one could find fault with him there.

As Ellie and Caroline came downstairs, Jane thought she heard the car returning. But going out, she was dismayed instead to see that McGregor had arrived and was wheeling the mower across the lawn, while his wife installed herself on the rug with Susan.

The active force of her own hate startled Jane.

"I'm going to issue an ultimatum to the McGregors," she said to Ellie. "Can you keep an eye on the kids for a couple of hours if I disappear after that? Donald's asleep."

"Of course, darling."

"I've just got to get away for a bit. I'll go to the afternoon service."

Jane walked into the garden again. McGregor had paused by his wife and was saying something to her in a low tone to which she was listening with her usual thin-lipped wary-eyed skeptical attention. Jane was therefore able to address them both together.

"I understand I've been doing you an injustice," she said to them coldly. "Naturally if I'd realized that you were my brother- and sister-in-law I'd have— things would have been quite different from the start. I can't understand why *you* didn't tell me, in fact."

"Oh, madam," McGregor said softly, but he was smiling. "It was hardly our place to tell you if Graham didn't choose to acknowledge us, was it?"

"However, now I *have* found out," Jane went on, ignoring him, "it makes it easier for me to say what I'm going to. This arrangement is quite unsuitable and has got to end, right away. Furthermore I don't want to see either of you, ever again. If—if you have reasonable claims on Graham, let me know, and I'll see they are settled—if we *can* settle them. We're not at all well off, you know."

"No?" said McGregor, smiling. "Still, you're better off than us, living in that filthy little den, down by the foot of the weir."

"But if you send any more anonymous letters," Jane went on, "or try to get money out of Graham by putting pressure on him, I shall tell the police. Blackmail is a criminal offence, you know."

"But madam—you have to consider Graham's point of view. Maybe there's things he hasn't told you that he'd rather people didn't get to hear? Things that would do him no good. You ask him about Hannastoul House, for instance. I don't suppose he told you about that?"

"The town clerk had a breakdown and was considered unfit to plead," Myfanwy said, fixing Jane with her pale eyes. "But he's better now, and Tim went to see him and found he had some letters still, that Graham wrote him seven years ago. I daresay Graham is sorry he wrote those letters now."

"I'm not interested in your malicious gossip," Jane said.

Hannastoul House? Why did that ring a bell? She went on as firmly as she could, "I'm going to church now, and when I come back, I shall expect to find that you've packed up all your things and gone."

She walked on, without waiting for an answer, leaving four coldly unwavering eyes fixed on her back. Through the overcast gray sky, a feeble sun was trying to shine. Susan, sitting on a patch of damp soil, raised an indifferent, vacant stare to the sky, and Jane suddenly shuddered, seeing a resemblance to Caroline at the times when she wore her abstracted, preoccupied expression. Of course they were cousins. No wonder McGregor sometimes looked at lively, active, bright-eyed Caroline the way he did.

When Jane reached the church, however, her intentions received a check. Afternoon service, she read on the sign pinned to the door, was this week being held at Five Oaks, the other church of the scattered parish. She would not be able to get there in time.

What to do instead? She could not return home at once; she must give the McGregors a decent margin to collect their stuff and leave. Go for a walk? But after last night's wakeful hours she was tired to the marrow of her bones.

The sound of the bus, slowly grinding its way up the hill, solved her problem. She ran up, reached the stop just before it did, swung herself on, and bought a ticket for the round trip. That would nicely fill up the time. And she could do with a period of peaceful, uninterrupted reflection.

Peaceful? Well, uninterrupted, anyway. She stared, unseeing, for the whole ride, out of the window at the gray-green sheaves of trees on the wooded ridge, at the mathematically ranged hop rows and sharp, prick-eared oast houses. There was no one on the bus but herself and the driver.

Presently it began to rain.

Tom, she thought once. If only I could have told Tom about it all. But it's too late now.

When she reached home, two hours later, it was raining hard. She had no coat and ran from the gate to the house, splashing through puddles on the sandy drive.

No one in the downstairs rooms.

"Ellie!" she called up the stairs, kicking off her sodden shoes in the front hall. "Shut the bathroom window, will you, like a love? It'll be coming in on that side."

No answer. Puzzled, she went up, shut the bathroom window (the rain *was* coming in), then looked into the guest room, the children's room, her room, Graham's study. Nobody. But a pile of newspapers in the study caught her eye—they were in the middle of the floor. old yellow dailies—the *Scotsman,* the *Glasgow Herald* —she had not seen them before.

A headline hit her eye: "PROSECUTIONS IN THE HAN-NASTOUL HOUSE CASE. Fraudulent subcontractors sentenced."

She moved some aside and saw, earlier, lower in the pile: "HANNASTOUL HOUSE DISASTER. Another tower block collapses. At least 25 feared dead."

Now she remembered about it. But she had been in Malta then; her father had been ill; the news story had not affected her closely. It had had no personal application.

In any case this was not the moment to begin thinking about Hannastoul House. Her immediate concern was to find Ellie and the children. Could they all have gone around to Miss Ames for tea? In that case, Ellie would have left a note somewhere. Jane ran downstairs again. A note would probably be on the kitchen counter—

She went into the kitchen and stopped short.

The McGregors were there, Tim leaning negligently against the stove, Mrs. McGregor upright and expressionless on a chair, Susan beside her.

"I told you to go," Jane said.

Where had they been when she first came in? Outside? Hiding?

"Oh, madam," McGregor said softly, "you wouldn't expect us to go off in all this rain, would you?"

His narrow black eyes slid over and past her, reached his wife, came back to Jane again.

Glancing out of the window, she noticed that the car was back in the garage. So Graham must be somewhere. The back door was ajar.

"Graham?" she called.

There was no answer. Where had everybody got to? "Graham?"

No answer.

A fear began to take hold of Jane.

"Mr. *Drummond* was out in the garden sunbathing," McGregor said, smiling. "Very keen on getting a tan, he is—always was, from a boy. He went out over an hour ago, hoping to get nice and brown. I shouldn't wonder but what he's still out there."

He nodded towards the far end of the garden. Jane, looking in this direction with disbelieving eyes saw something—a black blob—Graham's head?—just appearing over the low rise that ran down to the line of willow trees. Was he lying on the grass in the pelting rain?

In two steps she was out through the back door. She

102

flew over the sodden grass, calling, "Graham! Graham! What *are* you doing?"

But really she knew all the time.

He was lying in a deck chair, his head flung back, his spine slightly arched, and his mouth open as if he were snoring. In fact it seemed likely that he had been asleep and snoring up to the moment when somebody had come up behind him and savagely thrust a long steel garden spike down through his gullet.

He was not a pleasant sight.

Caroline, was Jane's first thought. At all costs she mustn't see this. But where is she, where are the children? Where's Ellie? I must find them. Telephone. Get the police.

Then, in the sodden, silvery, long grass beyond Graham's chair, she saw a line of footprints leading down the hill to the fence and the line of willows. They were small prints, the high heels had sunk into the soft soil here and there. They went down the hill; they did not come back.

Ellie?

Jane started towards the weir, lead-colored under the weeping sky; then hesitated. There was only one line of footprints. Where were the children?

She ran back to the house, thinking, Nobody, nobody could possibly stick a thing down their own throat like that. Therefore what has happened to Graham is murder.

She saw the word in black capitals like a newspaper headline.

Hurrying in through the front door, leaving it open, she went straight into the sitting room, to the telephone, regardless of the trail of black wet footprints she left across the pale carpet and of her wet dress dripping on the green chair.

The McGregors came through silently from the kitchen as she began to dial.

"I wouldn't do that if I was you," McGregor said gently. "Not just yet."

He took the receiver from her hand and replaced it on the cradle.

"What do you mean?" Jane stared at him.

She had come straight into the house without reflection, because her first thought had been to get to the nearest phone. Now she regretted that she had not run down the hill to the phone booth outside the post office. There was a powerful threat in the silence of the McGregors. It came to her in a chill flash that they were two against her one.

Graham—Was it possible *they* could have done it? She could not contemplate his death.

"Your husband's dead, isn't he," McGregor said softly. "Do you know who killed him?"

"I—"

Jane hesitated. She began to appreciate the danger of her position. She glanced about, wondering what they would do if she walked briskly back through the front door. But the children? Where were the children?

As if reading her thought, McGregor spoke.

"I expect you want to know where your children are," he said. "We've got them. Not here. At our place. My wife and I took them away while you were out. It wasn't really very sensible to go off like that, riding on the bus, was it? Quite a silly thing to do. People could easily say you neglected your kids, just going off that way and leaving them. Myfanwy saw you get on the bus. She thought it rather peculiar, since you'd said you were going to church. Quite annoyed about it, she was. When Myfanwy's in a real passion, it takes her funny ways."

"Who killed my husband?" said Jane, looking at him straight. "Did you?"

His voice when he replied was hardly louder than a coal shifting in the fire. "Why, madam, you killed him yourself. Myfanwy and I saw you do it."

"You know that's a lie," Jane breathed. "How could you possibly hope to get away with it?"

"Not if you wrote a confession, saying you'd done it?"

"I wouldn't be very likely to do that." Jane spoke carefully, warily, placing each word like a cautious foot on swampy ground.

"Oh, I think you would." The narrow black eyes were smiling. It was not an agreeable smile. "After all, you have to think of the children now, don't you? What's going to happen to them? We shall tell our story. A murderess's children live under a bit of a cloud, don't they? I'm afraid they won't get such a good start in life as you had—or clever Graham, with all his A-levels and his scholarships."

"What have you done with them?" And now Jane was verging on panic. She tried not to let it emerge, but her voice shook. "Where are they?"

"At our bungalow, I told you. You've never been there, have you, madam? Didn't find it worth your while to come and call. Well, and why should you? It's not very nice. Not like this. Not a good part of the village; no reason why you should ever go that way. Very close to the weir; always fussing you were, weren't you, about the children getting down to it; quite a carry-on, you used to make. Well, they're a good deal closer now. I'm afraid I had to lock the kids in the scullery. It's the only room with a bolt on the door, and it'll be a bit dark by now, as there's no electricity. We're used to roughing it, of course, not like you and my brother."

"Bring them back at once!" said Jane furiously. "If you don't I'll—"

She started swiftly towards the door, but McGregor was even faster. With the stealth and speed of a puma he put himself in her way.

"Oh, no, madam. Not just yet. First you have to sign the confession saying you did in your husband because you found out he was having it off with your friend—with Miss Rostrevor. Meeting at the Little White Rock Hotel, Hastings."

"As if I'd do such a thing. What an idiotic tale. It's not true." But a sudden dreadful qualm took the certainty from her voice.

"Oh, but it is true, madam. And she was carrying his baby. Myfanwy heard them having a bit of an argument about it last night. Well, more of a quarrel, really. People will find it quite easy to believe you had a grudge against her and him. I really think you had better write that confession. Hadn't she, Myfanwy?"

At that, Jane turned to look at Mrs. McGregor, who had remained silent all this time, watching, with her pale unblinking eyes fixed on Jane's face.

"Not so high and mighty now, are you?" she said, and the triumphant hate in her voice was like a knife suddenly drawn across flesh. "I was just the char to you, wasn't I? the daily? Yes, madam, and no, madam, and did Miss Caroline fancy her dinner and how did Miss Caroline come to dirty her frock? That rotten little, spoilt grizzling piece who can't even keep herself clean and dry. Not fit to be asked in for a cup of tea, were we? So stuck-up and proud you were, going out riding on the *bus*, rather than speak civil to us, although McGregor was putting your garden into shape and I was keeping your house decent."

Keeping her eyes fixed on Jane all the time, she

106

flicked a bit of mud off her shoe and ground it with her toe into the blond carpet. (Still six more payments on that, Jane though irrelevantly.) "White carpets! I'll give you white carpets, my fine lady. When we can't even afford oilcloth. Things are going to be a bit different now. You think this house is yours, don't you? Well, it's not. It belongs to the people who've worked on it, Tim and me. Who got the garden going? Who kept the place clean? Not you and that bit of trash you called your husband!"

"Look—you're talking rubbish," said Jane, trying to steady the banging of her heart. Mrs. McGregor's eyes were unnaturally bright; her voice had the flat, high, singsong note of paranoia.

"Oh, no, it's not rubbish, my lady. And I'll tell you another thing you maybe don't know. Graham was married to my sister before he ever met you—maybe you think he was too classy to be married to any sister of mine—"

"Of course not. I knew he was—"

"And he loved Ceridwen more than he ever loved *you,* let me tell you, only she couldn't have children. If she had—they'd have been a sight better than those brats of yours—"

"Myfanwy's not just very fond of your children," her husband murmured in his gentle voice. "A bit mardy, she found them—Caroline specially. Better for a good hiding or two she'd be, Myfanwy reckons. Myfanwy misses her sister badly, you see. Got killed, she did, when Hannastoul House collapsed—that block Graham designed. He had a flat there, and she was in it that night. Bled to death under a girder."

"If he'd been there as he ought, he could have got her out," Mrs. McGregor said tonelessly. "Or he'd have been killed, too, which would have been a bloody good job. But oh, no, clever Mr. Graham wasn't spending much time in that block; he was the expert; he knew too much about it. He was off on one of his trips to Malta, fixing to start a new life for himself when he'd got rid of his barren wife and his low connections.''

"I don't understand a thing you're talking about," Jane said blankly. "Graham designed Hannastoul House?"

"He designed it. My firm put it up. I was doing well in those days. Gorbals Contractors. Graham wasn't too proud to work with his family in those days," McGregor said.

Jane wondered how, after a prison sentence at nineteen, McGregor had achieved his own building firm. But perhaps Graham had helped him.

"Then, when trouble came, things were a bit different," Myfanwy said between her teeth. "When the trouble came, you couldn't see our fine Mr. Graham for dust. Then it was Tim who had to carry the can again and go to prison while Mister Graham got off scot-free, quite exonerated, no blame attached. Said he knew nothing whatever about it. Only we knew different. So he went to Malta and changed his name, so he wouldn't be remembered in connection with the scandal."

Yes, of course. Jane remembered a bit more about the case. It had been proved that the subcontractors were aware of the faulty building methods and inferior construction materials; but the architect had been completely cleared.

"Well," she said stoutly, "who's going to be such a fool as to design something that will fall down?"

"When his own brother was running the job? Don't make me laugh," said Mrs. McGregor mirthlessly. "You can't tell *me* that wasn't why he took the flat and

108

left Ceridwen there. He'd got sick of her; he reckoned that was the best chance to get rid of her—"

"Stop it, Myfanwy," McGregor suddenly said. His tone was not loud, but it was tight as a bowstring. "You're starting to talk foolish again; you're not in control of yourself."

And it was true, a blob of spit had formed at each corner of Myfanwy's mouth; her hands were drily, soundlessly working over and over each other as if they longed to grab and grapple with something, to bend it and break it. "Get off home, now," her husband ordered her. "Children's bedtime, it is."

"I don't believe you've got the children at all," Jane said. "I left them with Miss Rostrevor. Where is she?"

"Miss Rostrevor wasn't quite herself, madam," McGregor said smoothly. He spoke with the satisfaction of someone who brings out the first of several aces. "Well, for a start, Graham came home, and they had words. Then she went upstairs and helped herself to a nip or two—she was on the bottle; you knew that. Bit unbalanced she was, one way and another; not the best person to leave in charge of your kids. Myfanwy went up and saw her at it—took two or three sleeping tablets she did, as well; then she went down and chucked herself into the weir."

Jane opened her mouth. Shut it again. Had Ellie killed Graham? Had she been pregnant? Was the story true?

It might be. Poor Graham. Poor, poor, wretched Graham. In debt, in difficulties, his past catching up with him, turning for hopeless comfort to his wife's best friend, and only sinking deeper into the bog.

"Want to come and see?" McGregor said. Apparently tired of inaction, he suddenly took her arm in

109

a punishing grip and, saying sharply over his shoulder, "Get on back, now, Myfanwy! You know what to do." He dragged Jane roughly out of the sitting room and upstairs.

She saw in Ellie's room what she had not assimilated before, on her rapid search, the empty whiskey flask, the half-empty bottle of sleeping pills, and a sheet of paper on which was written, "Jane—sorry—dungeon—"

"Not herself at all," McGregor remarked consideringly. "It was you told her where the sleeping tablets were kept, wasn't it? Last night when she went to bed, I happened to be just outside the kitchen window. Forgot my hacksaw and had to come back for it. Ah, no"— as Jane put out her hand for the paper—"we don't want to go destroying evidence or covering up fingerprints, do we?"

He still had tight hold of Jane's arm, and with the same effortless strength—from all those hours of mowing, digging, and planning, she thought—he swung her around and out through the door which he locked, pocketing the key.

"We'll fetch in the police by and by, when you've written that confession," he said.

Jane stumbled on their return progress down the stairs, and he jerked her sharply against the newel post, jarring her arm and shoulder, bruising her cheek. The veneer of false deference had amused him for a long time, but it was finally wearing thin.

The downstairs part of the house was empty and silent now. Mrs. McGregor had gone.

Jane had a sudden unbearable picture of the baby in his pram, Caroline crouched beside him, in a dark squalid little scullery in an empty house—not far from the weir—waiting for Mrs. McGregor's return.

With a burst of despairing energy, she twisted from McGregor's grasp and ran for the front door.

But it was locked. She doubled through the kitchen. McGregor was after her with silent, swift efficiency; he tripped her, and she fell full-length on the black and red tiles.

He knelt beside her, pinning her easily with one knee, and tied her hands, using a length of garden bast which he drew from his pocket, taking his time, making a careful job of it. The stuff cut into her wrists.

Then he dragged her upright, sat her on a stool, and they looked at one another.

"The moment you agree to write what I tell you, I'll undo them," he said, nodding at her bound wrists, breathing a little quickly, otherwise not at all discomposed by the struggle.

"You'll never get away with such a load of lies," Jane said. "There must be dozens of clues—fingerprints, witnesses. Anyway I was on the bus at the time Graham was killed. I must have been. The driver will be able to confirm that."

"Not Dick Horsmonden," said McGregor, chuckling. "There was only you and him on the bus, wasn't there? So Myfanwy said. And I know much too much about what he does in the twenty-minute break at Ickfield; no, *he* won't help you. He'll say what I tell him to say— that you got off the bus at Fern Hill and walked home across the fields by the footpath. You could do it easy in twenty minutes. Fingerprints are easy to deal with, too. And the only person who might argue is Miss Rostrevor, and she's in the weir."

"I don't believe you," Jane said; but she did.

"Her doing that was quite convenient, really."

This is like the worst kind of dream, Jane thought.

Here I sit, in my own kitchen, listening to a man telling me that Ellie is dead and that her death was quite convenient. There must be some way in which I can get help. Someone who'd believe me. Neighbors—the police —*would* they believe me? Tom?

With his unnerving talent for guessing her thought, McGregor said, "People round here knew you and your husband didn't get on, you know. Myfanwy's quite a one for a bit of chat in the post office. And there was lots noticed how friendly you were with Mr. Roland, slipping out to meet him at the China Bowl, coming home in his motor every day. Who knows where you'd been spending the day together? You know how tongues wag in a village. Lots of people were sure there was something funny going on."

No, not Tom. I couldn't involve him in all this. It must be the police.

The telephone rang.

"Answer it," said McGregor.

He shoved her into the next room, and held the receiver against her mouth and ear.

"Help!" shouted Jane.

"Oh, it's not the least bit of use shouting help, madam," said Mrs. McGregor's voice. "I was just ringing up to say that I've got home now. Back to the bungalow. Miss Caroline's been a naughty girl—she was wet and dirty again—and I've had to larrup her. I'm afraid she'll have to go in the outside coal hole unless she improves. Perhaps you'd like to speak to her, madam, tell her to be a better girl?"

"I don't believe you've got them there at all," Jane gasped.

"Do you want to hear her voice? Wait just a minute. I'll fetch her."

There came a pause; then she heard the sound of a

brisk smack, and Mrs. McGregor's voice, fierce but farther off, whispering, "Say hullo, Mummy, you little flamer, or I'll give you such a tanning—"

A faint, tearful voice said, "Hullo, Mummy."

"Caroline? Is that really you? Is Donald there? Are you at Mrs. McGregor's?"

"Hullo, Mummy," the voice said again. There was a scuffling, bumping sound. Mrs. McGregor said, "Oh, you little madam—" and Jane heard a stifled cry. Then a click and silence.

"You see you really had better sit down and write what I tell you," McGregor said. "Here's a ballpoint and some paper."

He pushed her into one of the green armchairs and put the paper, laid on top of a flat coffee-table artbook, in her lap.

"I, Jane Drummond, confess that I murdered my husband, Graham, when I found out that he was carrying on with my friend Ellie, and when she saw what I'd done, she went and chucked herself in the weir—"

Jane sat, staring at the paper.

"Why are you doing this?" she said wearily.

"For the house."

"But—what difference to you will my confession make?"

"Just to be sure no one thinks I had a hand in it, as I'm next of kin," he said, smiling. "I shall lie low for a while—for a year, maybe two or three even— till it's all blown over. Then I'll turn up and claim the estate. No one need know that I was McGregor the gardener; I needn't come anywhere near here. It won't make any difference to you; you'll be in prison, and the children in an orphanage. Unless, of course," he added slowly, "you'd like me and Mfyanwy to look after them. After all, I am their uncle."

Here he had gone too far, and he knew it. Jane drew back.

"If it's the house you're after, nothing I write is going to do you a bit of good," she said.

After all, Donald is Graham's direct heir, she was going on to say, but checked the words. Donald? A six-month-old baby left alone in the little house by the weir with Mrs. McGregor nurturing paranoid resentment over the death of her sister?

She said instead, "None of it's paid for. The house is mortgaged up to the maximum."

"There was the deposit," McGregor said quickly. "And Graham's life insurance policy."

"Graham had raised money on that as well. Even if you did inherit, I solemnly promise you, the only assets you could realize are my own and the children's clothes. All the furniture's being bought on hire purchase."

Then McGregor did curse, long and softly and obscenely.

"I told that *bloody* stupid bitch how it would be," he muttered. "I *said* he'd be a lot more use to us alive. But she got so worked up and angry after you were rude to her and gave her notice to quit, she was just crazy to get her hands on Graham—"

She? Her hands?

And then Jane remembered vaguely noticing that Mrs. McGregor's hands, working over and over each other, were curiously stained, curiously dark and dirty in color.

Suppose I pretend to give in, she thought, what then? I didn't manage to get away from him before, but it seems the only hope.

By now it was dusk. She could hardly see his expression, for he had his back to the window. His eyes

114

were simply two black holes in the mask of his face. But something in his motionless, expectant attitude told her the truth:

He's never going to let me go. I'll never get out of here alive.

Cheated of the money, his hate would seize on this last outlet.

"If I sign," she said, "will you agree to do something for the children?"

Deliberately she let the tears of exhaustion and helplessness, which she had been holding back, run down her cheeks. She fumbled with her bound hands for the pen.

"Oh, certainly. I wouldn't let Graham's children starve," McGregor said, "anymore than he let me starve." He laughed gently. "You are going to write then? I'll just make you a bit more secure."

He stooped and, with another length of bast, tied her ankles savagely tight, then, with a swift slash of a pruning knife, cut the strands around her wrists.

Obediently she took up the pen.

His eyes followed her fingers, moving slowly: *I, Jane Drummond* . . .

"Killed my husband," McGregor said.

. . . and if that article on karate was inaccurate, Jane thought, I shall probably never read an illustrated weekly again. With a full swing of her right arm, she brought her hand edgewise against his throat and, following her advantage, levered herself up and drove an elbow desperately hard into his chest.

The pruning knife spun out of his hand, falling on the carpet. She heard him choke, and a chair went crashing against the french window as he recovered his balance. She groped for the knife—snatched it, managed to cut the string around her ankles, but now he was up again and had her by the arm in a numbing grip. The knife dropped out of her hand. She struggled and twisted, but knew already that it was hopeless.

Then she heard a lot more breaking glass. There were lights, shouts, and the thud of numerous feet. Someone shouted her name, "Janey! Are you all right?"

Somebody switched on the overhead light. She had an instantaneous glimpse of McGregor's face—which was to haunt her at moments for the rest of her life—before he ran for the inner door. Several large dark forms went after him.

Unexpectedly Jane found herself back lying in the armchair. She tried to struggle out of it again, but one of her own teacups was under her nose, full of brandy—they must have found the bottle kept for medicinal uses.

"Drink it up, Janey."

That was Tom. What was he doing here?

She coughed over the brandy's stinging warmth.

"The children—Donald and Caroline," she said gasping, pushing away the cup. "That awful woman has got them—they're at her bungalow—she may be doing God knows what to them. I think she's mad—"

"No, she hasn't got them, Janey. They're at my house. D'you want to come along there now?"

With unexpected strength, he hoisted her to her feet and turned, addressing some dark-blue uniformed character with a lot of stripes and gold buttons. "Look, Super, can I get her away from here? Is it all right to take her to my house? You can come and talk to her just as well there—Better."

"Yes, of course, Mr. Roland. We'll run you both over in the police Jag. Bring it up to the house, will you, Denny?"

116

Time was all fractured for Jane, like the splintered french window; it expanded and contracted; nothing seemed to join together. There was an immense interval—it might have been two hours—while she stood supported by Tom's arm—then a lightning-quick sequence in a dark car which was crackling all the time with radio conversations; then she was in Tom's house, where she had never been before.

A big, comfortable room, books on two walls, a grand piano, Swedish rugs, a wide stone hearth. Caroline, Peter Anstey, and Miss Ames sitting by the fire. Donald's pram in a dim corner.

Jane was beyond speech. She ran in and knelt by Caroline, gathering the child in her arms.

"We had a lovely party, Mummy," Caroline said importantly. "First of all, Ellie took us over to tea at Miss Ames, and then we came to Mr. Roland's to play games. Where's Ellie? She said she'd be back in five minutes, but she never did come back."

"She—she didn't feel well, darling. That was why she didn't come back."

Jane looked up, white-faced, at Tom. Her mouth shaped the word, "Weir."

The smile left Tom's face. He turned and said something in a low voice to the police officer who had accompanied them, then came back to Jane.

"Your friend" (she heard the reserve on the word in his voice) "took them around to Miss Ames, left them, said she was going back to fetch something, and didn't return. Miss Ames became a bit anxious, specially when later on Mrs. McGregor arrived and demanded the children. It all seemed a bit queer to her, particularly as she doesn't much like Mrs. McGregor. So she wouldn't let her take them. I happened to come in to the café for cigarettes just then, and I thought it

117

sounded pretty dicey, too. Mrs. McGregor was so angry, and so bent on taking the children; said you'd gone off on a bus ride and left them in her charge. Well, in the end, as Miss Ames couldn't leave the café, I persuaded her to let Peter and me bring them over here, and she said she'd come over when she'd finished serving teas.

"After she got here, Peter and I thought we'd better come around to your house to find out what went on. We came in on a bit of McGregor's coercion technique —heard it through the sitting-room window—so Peter bolted back to call the police and I stayed. It was a bit of an effort keeping mum, considering the sort of things he was saying, but I thought that unless he actually started in to use violence, it would be useful for the cops to catch him *in situ*."

"Miss Ames," Jane said. "I just don't know how to thank you for not letting them go with that—that woman."

"Who? That Mrs. McGregor? Not likely," said Miss Ames stoutly. "Why, she's a blackmailer! Tried to get ten shillings a week from me once, saying she'd tell the police I stole books from Corbett's bookshop."

"How wicked! As if you'd do such a thing!"

"Oh, I do all the time, bless you. Corbett's don't mind. I take the books back when I've read 'em. And I give them eggs and cakes in exchange. Between you and me, I think that Mrs. McGregor's off her head, though; she has a really nasty look in her eyes sometimes."

There was a long, exhausted pause. Time slipped past again. Jane found herself on a sofa, with her feet up, sipping hot milk with brandy in it.

"No, really, I'm sure I shouldn't, if I'm to talk to the police—"

"Here they are now," Tom said. He seemed to appear and disappear, flickeringly, like a genie out of a bottle. "Can you manage it all right?"

"Did they find—Ellie?" Jane asked, hesitating in the doorway.

He nodded, holding her arm, looking down at her, suddenly grave.

"Did you *know*—about her and Graham?"

"Would that make it easier to bear? Yes. I'd seen them, you see—at a hotel in Hastings. Graham was very put out at my accidentally running into them. He introduced her as his sister-in-law."

"Oh, poor Graham. Poor silly Graham."

"THAT MESSAGE ELLIE WROTE ON THE BIT OF PAPER," JANE said to the superintendent of police. "I don't think she was unbalanced when she wrote it. I think it meant something. When we were at school together, a *dungeon* was our name for a secret hiding place under a loose floorboard. We used to keep sweets there. In the guest-room at Weir View there's a loose board; I showed it to Ellie myself, just for fun, when I first took her up to her room."

"I'll tell my men to have a look, Mrs. Drummond."

UNDER THE LOOSE BOARD THEY FOUND HALF A SHEET OF paper.

Ellie had written, "Jane, it's no use saying I'm sorry. You're the only real friend I ever had, and I did you dirt. But Graham was no good. You'll be better

119

without him, honestly. I saw Mrs. McG kill him with spike. She's crazy I think. From window. G. had told me to get out, wouldn't let me stay in the house. Couldn't leave C & D here with that woman. They're with Miss A. I'm just no good, never shall be. All I do is cause trouble. So I'm going to finish now before giving you any more. Sorry, sorry, Jane dear. . . ."

Mrs. McGregor and Susan were never found.

"She must have seen the game was up when Miss Ames wouldn't part with your kids, and I was there, taking too much interest," Tom said. "She very likely sneaked back to your house to tell McGregor, saw me or Peter or the cops, and bunked."

"Then that phone call was a trick; it must have been Susan's voice," said Jane, shivering as she remembered it. "I suppose it was from the phone booth in the village. If I'd thought for a minute, I might have known they wouldn't have a telephone at the bungalow."

"They were best at bluff, the McGregors. Hate is a great drive, but it doesn't make for efficiency. That whole confession idea wouldn't have stood up for a moment in court if you'd decided to go back on it."

"No, I could see that," Jane said. "So I knew he must really be planning to kill me and fake it to look like suicide—dump me in the weir, too, most likely,"

"You realized that—"

"It was the look in his eyes," she said slowly. "I could see he wouldn't be happy till he'd done for me. I suppose because of how he felt towards Graham."

"Graham had succeeded where he had failed."

"Or so he thought," Jane said sadly. "It was a shock when he learned that the whole façade was nothing but a mass of debt and make-believe.—I shall have to get a permanent job now, all right."

"I can offer you one."

"As a daily woman?"

"Not daily. Permanent. But we won't talk about it just yet, shall we?"

She shook her head. "What'll happen to McGregor?"

"Oh—a sentence. Demanding money with menaces. Accessory before the fact. Lots of motives. Lots of past history. It won't be very nice, Janey."

"It doesn't matter. The children are all right—that's all that counts."

They were sitting in Miss Ames's front parlor, while Miss Ames made gingerbread men for Caroline and Caroline helped. Jane had not been able to go back to Weir View, not even for a night. Miss Ames had calmly taken them in; later on, she said, Jane could help in the café in exchange, if she felt like it, when she was back on her feet.

Caroline bustled in from the kitchen to exhibit a pan full of shapeless dough objects. "Look, look, Mummy. Look what I made! We're going to bake 'em now."

When they had been praised and exclaimed over and put in the oven, Caroline wandered across to the window and drew a finger down the tracks of the raindrops outside.

"I'm going out with Miss Ames to pick dandelion leaves for tea when it stops raining, Mummy. We're going along to Mallam Woods, and we're going to take Donald in the pram. But do you think it ever *is* going to stop raining?"

"Oh, yes," said Tom. "Don't you despair. By and by, it will."

JOAN AIKEN, WELL KNOWN IN A DOZEN COUNTRIES FOR HER mystery thrillers, has published nearly a score of books for adults and juveniles alike.

Daughter of the poet Conrad Aiken, and sister of two professional writers, she was born in England, and began writing at the age of five, because, as she says, "writing is just the family trade."

Her varied career includes work with the United Nations in London, a stint in advertising, and a number of stories published in such magazines as *Vogue,* and *Ellery Queen's Mystery Magazine.* The author of such modern classics as *The Wolves of Willoughby Chase, Black Hearts in Battersea* and *Nightbirds on Nantucket,* Miss Aiken has won the prestigious Manchester Guardian Award for Children's Literature. And her recent *The Whispering Mountain* was chosen runner-up for the Carnegie Medal for children's literature.

The mother of two children, Joan Aiken now lives in Sussex, England, where, in addition to writing, she paints, gardens, and collects 19th century children's literature. Her frequent walks in the English countryside have led her to some of the haunting places which reappear in her books.